MEMENTO NORA

MEMENTO NORA

BY ANGIE SMIBERT

Marshall Cavendish

Other Marshall Cavendish Offices: Marshall Cavendish International (Asia) Private
Limited, 1 New Industrial Road, Singapore 536196 • Marshall Cavendish International
(Thailand) Co Ltd. 253 Asoke, 12th Flr, Sukhumvit 21 Road, Klongtoey Nua, Wattana,
Bangkok 10110, Thailand • Marshall Cavendish (Malaysia) Sdn Bhd, Times Subang,
Lot 46, Subang Hi-Tech Industrial Park, Batu Tiga, 40000 Shah Alam, Selangor Darul
Ehsan, Malaysia

Marshall Cavendish is a trademark of Times Publishing Limited

Library of Congress Cataloging-in-Publication Data
Smibert, Angie.
Memento Nora / by Angie Smibert.
p. cm.
Summary: In a near future in which terrorism is commonplace but memories of
horrors witnessed can be obliterated by a pill, teens Nora, Winter, and Micah create
an underground comic to share with their classmates the experiences they want to
remember.
ISBN 978-0-7614-5829-6
[1. Memory—Fiction. 2. Government, Resistance to—Fiction. 3. Cartoons and comics—
Fiction. 4. Terrorism—Fiction. 5. Science fiction.] I. Title.
PZ7.S63986Mem 2011
[Fic]—dc22
2010011816

This novel began as a short story: "Memento Nora" published in ODYSSEY magazine,
May/June 2008, © 2008 Carus Publishing. Used with permission.

Book design by Virginia Pope
Editor: Marilyn Brigham

Printed in China (E)
10 9 8 7 6 5 4 3 2 1

 Marshall Cavendish

To my mother, who always wanted to be a writer

Nothing to See Here

Therapeutic Statement 42-03282028-11
Subject: JAMES, NORA EMILY, 15
Facility: HAMILTON DETENTION CENTER TFC-42

I'm about to forget everything I'm going to tell you. So I'm only going to mention the parts that matter. To you, at least. The rest I'm going to keep to myself, for my self. For that old Nora James. The obedient daughter. The popular girl. The oblivious consumer. The one who really owns this cute little charm bracelet with the silver purse dangling from it. The one you want to keep around.

It all started a few weeks ago. It was a glossy day. No school. Downtown was having a sale to celebrate two quiet weeks in a row. And Mom was in one of her good moods—her post-TFC mood—and generous with the credit. A very glossy day.

We bought strappy sandals at Macy's, a cute leather jacket at Bergdorf's, and ice cream, low-fat chocolate mint, at Burkes. Then we were going to Fahrenheit Books for coffee and a new romance novel for Mom. We were doing our part to prime our feeble economy, as Dad likes to say, while the security patrol watched over us from their machine-gun nest atop Saks.

As we were walking down Market Street, there was a noise like a hundred Fourth of Julys. A body thudded onto the concrete about twenty feet in front of us. It rattled like a bag of bones as it hit the sidewalk. Mom turned me away, but not before I saw it was a man in a dark suit. Brooks Brothers, I think. He had no shoes on, just red socks; but he still had a book clutched in his hand, the hand with a silver watch on it. Burned paper fell from the sky and covered the sidewalk in a thick blanket of ash. Car alarms rang up and down the street. The air smelled like that bonfire we had last fall before Homecoming.

And that's when I noticed that the top of Fahrenheit Books, the history and classics section, had blown right off. I knew it was history and classics because of the charred books at my feet. *The Art of War*. *The Fall of the Roman Empire*. *Medieval Churches*. In the back of my nonglossy mind, I wondered which book had been the last thing imprinted on the dead guy's brain.

Security pointed their automatic weapons at us and herded everyone back into the stores. "Nothing to see here," they shouted. Then a black helicopter rose over Bergdorf's and swept down the block.

Everyone Knows About TFC

Therapeutic Statement 42-03282028-11
Subject: JAMES, NORA EMILY, 15
Facility: HAMILTON DETENTION CENTER TFC-42

That night I had the dream.

The body fell like a leaf in a rain of stinging ash. Mom covered my eyes, but I still heard it hit the pavement, still heard the bones rattle, still saw those red socks. This time I could see that his silver watch had stopped at ten past two. I couldn't make out the book title. Gray covered everything. I wiped and wiped, but nothing came clean. I was so not glossy.

Someone tousled my hair.

"Nora, wake up," Mom said quietly. "It's just a dream."

I shook my head. It felt real.

"Go back to sleep," Mom told me. "That memory will be gone by lunch tomorrow. And then we'll go shopping."

But I couldn't get back to sleep. The memory wouldn't

let go. Everything in that moment was flash frozen in my brain. Every little detail.

Fumbling for the light on my nightstand, I sent something clattering to the floor. A cold, dark skin of chocolate with tiny, bright red eruptions of cinnamon sprinkles oozed across the wood. I hadn't touched the cocoa Dad had brought me before bed. Like always, he'd wanted me to talk about what was bothering me—what I'd seen—but all I'd wanted to do was turn up the Bag Boys on my earbuds really loud and stick my head under my pillow.

It hadn't helped. Still, I gave it one more shot. I laid there, lights on, cocoa drying on the floor, listening to the Boys' "Glossy Girl" until the alarm rang.

*　　*　　*

During breakfast, Mom had one of those morning 'casts on in the kitchen. The hosts were comparing new fat-reducing products. I picked at my egg while I watched.

The blond guy concluded that the Reducal implant was the most effective one. "It'll suck the fat right out of those thighs, Diane."

The thin woman flashed him a fake smile, and then she turned to the screen. "To recap our top stories: the Coalition took credit for the Market Street bombing in downtown Hamilton yesterday as well as several others in the Mid-Atlantic region. Washington, Philadelphia, Charlotte, Wilmington, all reported—"

Mom flicked off the screen.

"We need to get going, honey," she said.

Dad bounded down the stairs in his usual hurry.

"My little girl is making her first visit to TFC." He pecked me on the cheek and then Mom. She flinched.

She dabbed makeup on her right cheekbone after he left.

Sentinel Car Service picked us up in front of our house in a glossy black SUV.

"TFC downtown," Mom told the driver.

As soon as the car pulled away from the curb, ads flickered across the blast-proof glass windows in the back. *Forget your cares at TFC*. The letters floated like clouds over a flock of sheep grazing in a lush green field. *Fifteen new locations opening soon* blinked in red across the bottom of the field. I didn't click the info icon. Everyone knows about TFC.

The ad cycled. A mother packed up a bunch of kids in soccer uniforms and drove out of the gates of a compound, all safe and snug in her new Bradley MPV. It looked like a tank. *Feel as safe as if you'd never left home*.

I wished we lived in a compound.

The next ad was the scent that the woman from my favorite 'cast, *Behind the Gates*, sells. Guarded. The perfume whiff made me sneeze.

And then the Nomura Pink Ice mobile came up. Very glossy. I clicked on that one and picked up the info on my mobile.

The Pink Ice was superslim, with a pearly pink body. You could do all the usual mobile things with it—watch 'casts, search the data stores, do homework, ID yourself, shop—but you could also lock it with a full retinal scan. And the

Pink Ice came with a sparkly case. I was sure I could talk the parentals into buying it for me.

"TFC, ma'am," the driver announced.

When we got out, a cop checked our IDs and warned us that a car had just exploded in front of Macy's. That's why everyone I know—who doesn't live in a compound— uses secure car services. That, Dad said, and because the insurance for owning a car is astronomical. Poor people, he explained, drive without insurance or take the bus, which isn't much safer.

"We'll go to a mall next time," Mom told me. "The security's better."

Her usual TFC was sandwiched between a frozen-yogurt shop and an ex-Starbucks. The coffee shop was boarded up, but rubble still clogged the sidewalk. Someone had spray painted a word across the plywood—*MEMENTO*—in fire engine red. I began to feel hot.

"I can spare some points for a sundae." Mom flashed her mobile in my face. I didn't catch the whole number, but her TFC point balance sure had a lot of zeroes after it. I knew she was saving up for something—a trip maybe—but she never said exactly. As we tiptoed through the debris, she rattled off how many points you need for frozen yogurt: 25. Movies: 100. Spray tans: 300. Mobiles: 3,000. Her chatter didn't drown out that dreary body-on-asphalt sound echoing inside my head.

My hand trembled as I pushed open the door. The white letters on the glass read THERAPEUTIC FORGETTING CLINIC No. 23. Inside, the air was cool, the music soft, and the colors bright. I felt glossier already. Mom headed straight for the counter and swiped her mobile. Number 174 lit up on her screen. The now-serving sign over the counter blinked 129.

Mom cleared her throat. "It's her first time," she said.

A frizzy head popped up from behind the counter. The lady it belonged to went all sad and smiley at me. She asked me questions, and I told her: *Nora James. Fifteen. No. Fahrenheit Books.* The lady asked me if I had an ID implant. I shook my head, and she motioned for me to swipe my mobile over the reader.

My mobile chimed. The message said, *Welcome to TFC, Nora James. You've just earned 500 points for your first visit! You'll earn 100 points for each subsequent one.* Then the screen displayed the number 175.

"Hon, watch the orientation video," the lady called as I followed Mom to a blue table by the door.

Every seat had its own flat screen, which is better than watching stuff on your mobile, even if you have one of those virtual 3-D displays. I played the orientation on my screen; Mom watched a home renovation show on hers. The orientation droned on about how powerful emotions, along with adrenaline, can etch a memory onto your brain, making it hard to function productively. Doctors used to call it post-traumatic stress disorder. Back then you had to put up with the nightmares and the panic attacks. Now you just pop a pill and go on like nothing ever happened.

The video ended. I scrolled through the games menu while the now-serving number crept up slowly.

When I got bored, I decided to play my own game.

Guess the trauma. It was easy. Those four were soldiers. They'd probably seen someone killed, or worse, in war or a Coalition attack. That girl staring at cartoons saw a car bombing. So did that guy with the ugly glasses.

Something blew up in the city all the time. Fifty people were here on a Thursday morning.

They went into that door dreary. They came out glossy.

I noticed this guy, maybe my age, watching me. He had stitches over his right eye and a broken arm. He angled his cast so I could read something written on it. That word again. *Memento*.

Another number was called, and his mother dragged him toward the treatment room door.

I looked up that word on my mobile. A memento, it said, is a reminder of the past. Then some gushy jewelry ad played. Man gives woman diamond earrings for their anniversary. *Remember each year as if it were the first*, the ad said.

Ten minutes later the guy came out trailing his mother. She hurried out the door. He stuck out his tongue at me. *Loser*, I thought, until I saw the white pill sitting on his pink tongue. He coughed into his hand. Then he mouthed the word *remember*, tapping his cast, and tossed the pill in the trash can.

I watched him leave. He wasn't glossy. He wasn't dreary, either. He was something else.

He was all there.

Our numbers were called. I followed Mom through that door, and we sat down in a cold, white room.

A chubby doctor, almost as white as the walls, walked in. Without looking up from his mobile, he said, "Ah, Mrs. James. Oh, and I see we have a first timer." He looked all sad and smiley at me, just as the frizzy-haired lady had. "You've watched the orientation, right?"

I nodded, though I doubted I could have passed a quiz on the material.

"Any questions?" He looked back at his screen.

"I have a test tomorrow," I said.

He looked up. "Don't worry about that. The pill doesn't affect those kinds of memories. Different part of the brain."

I must have looked unconvinced.

"Okay," he said, putting down his pad on his desk. "I might as well give you my new-patient spiel." He laughed, more to himself than to us.

Great. A lecture.

"Our brains distinguish between emotional and other types of memories. When you experience fear—or any strong emotion—your body excretes adrenaline. That's what makes your heart race when you're scared. Adrenaline also opens up your brain cells." He held out his chubby pink hands palms up, fingers splayed, as if waiting for something to fall into them. "Your brain cells are ready to snatch up that event and make strong connections between one another." He meshed his fingers together and tugged. "Voilà. A traumatic memory."

He held a hard knot of fat, pink, wriggling fingers in front of me.

"Ameliorol—this pill I'm going to give you—keeps that from happening." His fingers slid apart. He shook them out as if they pained him. "I'm sure this kind of memory had some evolutionary advantage in our species, but frankly, it doesn't pay to remember that kind of thing today." He smiled rather sadly in my general direction.

"Wouldn't it work better if you gave me the pill right after the thing happened?" I asked.

"Yes, it would, young lady." He looked at me, impressed. "But you see, that memory isn't permanently stuck in your brain. Every time you replay that event in your head—or out loud—the memory has to stick itself to your nerve cells all over again.

"Ameliorol disrupts the resticking process. When you reactivate the memory, which is usually an emotional process, the chemicals in the pill bind to your nerve cells—temporarily—blocking the adrenaline from attaching and the memory from re-forming. It's fast acting and only affects emotional or traumatic memory. All that cramming for an exam gets stored elsewhere in your brain."

"Will I remember this part?" I asked. "You? The TFC?"

"Since this is your first visit, and you're nervous, the adrenaline is probably coursing through your veins and getting those brain cells ready to make a pretty vivid snapshot of right now. The pill will make the memory of your visit a wee bit fuzzy. You may remember the boring parts. Like the waiting room. And my little science lecture." His smile seemed genuine now.

"And since you're a minor, we not only like you to

be accompanied by a parent or guardian for the first time"—he turned to Mom—"but we also like said parent or guardian to set an example, when possible."

Mom swallowed hard and clutched her Louis Vuitton purse in front of her.

"Don't worry, Mrs. James," he said almost kindly. "The young lady won't remember what you say."

She nodded, still clutching her purse.

"Please describe the event you wish to erase," the chubby doctor said more briskly. "This will activate the memory so the drug will work appropriately," he told me. Then he added some standard legal blah-blah-blah about the session being recorded for our protection.

Mom started talking. I braced myself to hear the gruesome details. The explosion. The body. The ash. Instead, Mom said something about Dad. This time he was angry with her for taking me downtown, for exposing his princess to the death and violence in the world, for letting me see what I saw. *Wife, you're always disappointing me*, he'd said. Then he'd called her a stupid cow and slammed her face into the door frame.

Mom looked as gray as I felt. She didn't look at me. She washed down the pill the doctor handed her with greedy gulps of water. Her face went slack. Glossy. Not all there.

Then the doctor turned to me. I told him about the body falling and the ash covering everything, but all the time I was thinking about Mom. And Dad. She came to the clinic at least once a week. Now I knew why. How long had this been going on? And this time it was because of me.

Would she have put up with her life if she remembered? Would anybody? Would I?

I stared at the white pill in the doctor's fat, pink hand.

"It doesn't hurt, Nora," Mom said. Her nonglossy smile told me I wasn't getting out of here without taking the pill.

I put it in my mouth and took a tiny sip of water.

On my way out of the clinic, I spat the pill in the trash can.

3

I Am Such a Douche

Therapeutic Statement 42-03282028-12
Subject: WALLENBERG, MICAH JONAS, 15
Facility: HAMILTON DETENTION CENTER TFC-42

It all started with a girl. Sure, I tagged some walls and boarded-up windows with a goofy word I'd found in some old art books. Memento is Latin for "remember," like a command. Remember! And Memento Mori is this kind of art that's supposed to remind you you're alive by reminding you that you can die. Memento Mori! Remember you must die! Crazy cool. Lots of skulls and shit. I thought it would be all rebellious and rage against the machine to graffiti it on some nice, clean, vertical surfaces.

And I did. I tagged that Home Security Depot billboard on Market Street the day the bookstore blew up. Actually, I tagged it before its pyrotechnic number. I was skating away from the scene of the crime—the billboard, not the bomb—when this black van sideswiped me. Broke my arm in two places. The van didn't have any plates or markings, and the windows were totally blacked out. When I told the cops in the emergency room about the van, they put away their mobiles and told Mom I ought to go to TFC. *For his own good*, they said. *He'll have nightmares.*

Mom buys that shit. I don't.

I've learned not to fight her on TFC, though. It does a lot of good for her patients, she says. She's a nurse. And she's seen people go either all manic or zombielike after something bad happens. She's always telling me about Mr. So-and-So at Sunny Oaks who still has night terrors decades after he saw the World Trade Center collapse because he refuses to take the pill. Or Mrs. Such-and-Such who was watching the news and saw her daughter's car slide into the San Francisco Bay when that plane struck the Golden Gate Bridge. So Mom insisted I go to TFC. She always insisted. Plus, we needed the points. And I planned to do what I've always done before—at least that I can remember—spit it out.

When in doubt, spit it out.

Damn. I wish I'd thought of that earlier. It would've made a killer T-shirt.

So there we were at TFC-23. Mom, still in her purple scrubs, tired and annoyed with the world. Me, sporting a fresh cast and five stitches above my eye from where I caught the hot dog cart with my head after the black van hit me. I was sketching this little kid watching the bloodiest cartoon I'd ever seen. Then I saw her come in.

Nora James.

I'd seen her in school plenty. She's one of the pretty,

bourgeois crowd. You know, the pretty people with money—but not quite enough money (or smarts) to be in a better school. The kind that look right past you if you're not in their clique.

Here she was, sitting with the rest of us losers, watching us like we were bugs. I couldn't resist messing with her head a little.

I got out my pens and wrote that word on my cast in bright red. I flipped it in her direction before I followed Mom into the treatment room.

I did the whole blah-blah-blah thing, telling the doc about getting hit by the van. Then I stuck the pill under my tongue. All the while I was thinking about that girl. I have to confess; I've always thought she was cute in this little-girl-lost kind of way. She's probably never had to sleep in a car in her life. I felt the pill lying under my tongue. And that's when I decided I'd really mess with her. Wake her up, you know.

Mom was out the door as soon as I sipped some water. I followed at a safe distance. And just as I was passing by that girl—and I was sure no one else was looking—I stuck out my tongue with the pill on it and mouthed "remember" all mysterious-like at her. Priceless. Those big green eyes of hers were as big as hubcaps though she was trying to play it cool. But I saw a glimmer of something else there, too. Disgust for me, yeah, but something more. Something that made me sorry I'd done it.

She looked at me like she *saw* me. Like I wasn't just some skater kid with delusions of artistic grandeur. I can't really explain it.

I tossed the pill in the trash can and ran to catch up to Mom just as the bus rolled to a stop.

Mom slumped into a seat by the window and closed her eyes. I slid in next to her. She'd pulled a double shift just so she could take me to TFC today. I felt bad that she didn't trust me to go by myself, but she was right. I wouldn't have bothered going. Still, I felt bad. Bad for Mom. Bad for Nora James. Bad for me for being such a douche all the time.

I stared at some government ad playing on the window by Mom's head. *Consumption is one of our freedoms*, it said. Then the ad flipped to one for Home Security Depot. They were having a sale on surveillance and spy cameras this week. One of the cameras looked just like a pair of expensive sunglasses. I clicked the icon, and the scene shifted to a backyard pool party. A woman wearing shades hands a man a plate of hot dogs. The tag line said, *Think your neighbor's not a Good Citizen? Capture the proof, and look good doing it.*

Okay, in the grand scheme of things, I wasn't the douche.

That ad rolled right into another government PSA, this one about the quote-unquote Coalition. *Anyone can be an extremist*, the bold type said as a sea of faces flashed by. Each one looked oh so innocent until they turned to the camera with a knowing, villainous smirk that said they wouldn't have any trouble blowing up your car or the occasional coffee shop.

The smirk dissolved into the ever-lovely face of Channel

5 Action News reporter Rebecca Starr. She is hot, especially when she's wearing a really tiny shirt. You can just see the hint of a tattoo—a tiger claw—reaching over her shoulder. I imagined the beast climbing up her back, one paw sunk into her shoulder, head turned and fangs bared, ready to fend off the world. *Today, the Coalition claimed responsibility for a hijacking attempt on a flight into Geneva. Press Secretary, Aurora Adams, renewed the president's call for stricter European regulations. . . .*

Blah-blah-blah. It all made me so tired. And didn't it seem odd that every so-called extremist in the world banded together into this Coalition thing? It came out of nowhere back when I was a baby—at least that's what Mrs. Brooks said. Some guy plowed a plane into the Golden Gate Bridge, and the Coalition took credit for it. Then shit started blowing up all over the place. The Coalition was like some supervillain syndicate or terrorist Legion of Doom, but no Justice League had arisen from the chaos to combat the baddies. No, it was like the superheroes had abandoned Gotham, and we citizens were just supposed to pop a pill and forget all about it, until the next time the villains struck our fair land.

Yet these baddies never seemed to do anything massively destructive anymore—they didn't seem bent on destroying the world. These days it was mostly car bombs and the occasional store. I'm not complaining. It's just hard to figure out what this Legion of Doom really wants. To make life suck even harder than it already does? For some people, at least.

And speaking of sucking, the next ad was for that soccer-mom war-wagon monstrosity called the Bradley. All of Black Dog Village could sleep in there—with room left over for the dog.

Then I had another thought—the kind that, believe me, doesn't happen often enough or soon enough to keep me out of trouble. The thought was this: what if Nora James tells someone I spit out the pill?

I can be such a douche sometimes.

I didn't know if they could do anything to me. You never know these days. And I didn't want my mom to find out. It would kill her to know she went to all this trouble for nothing.

When we got home, I called my friend Winter to see what she thought. She thought I was a douche, too.

I can always count on Winter to back me up.

4

Remember the Milestones in Her Life

Therapeutic Statement *42-03282028-11*
Subject: *JAMES, NORA EMILY, 15*
Facility: *HAMILTON DETENTION CENTER TFC-42*

As we walked past the old Starbucks, I stumbled over a piece of broken concrete. Catching myself on the window, I came face-to-face with the graffiti again, that word, *MEMENTO*, in bright red paint, the color of socks, sprawling across the graying plywood. I wondered if the kid with the broken arm had done it. Or if he'd just copied it onto his cast.

I also wondered, as I eased into the backseat of the car, another green-field blue-sky TFC ad staring me in the face, how I was going to even look at my father when he got home. I could barely look at Mom sitting next to me, so relaxed, reading an old romance novel from the beginning. I knew I had to act glossy. Otherwise they'd know I knew. And how could I have not known something so huge? Staring at the fluffy white sheep dotting the green TFC field, I did think about going back, maybe to another clinic, confessing it all and taking the pill.

The ads changed about a half-dozen times on the way home, but I couldn't have told you what they were.

"Arlington Court, ma'am," the driver announced.

Again someone—this time the Home Defense guy, the rent-a-cop hired by the homeowners' association—scanned our mobiles. We walked up to our house in silence. Mom lagged behind as if she were trying to enjoy the scenery. We do live in a pretty area. Eighteenth-century town houses in alternating blues and creams and grays. Tree-lined streets with big oaks and maples forming a canopy over the pavement. Cobblestone sidewalks.

"So empty," she said, sad. She pulled her coat tight around her and walked a little faster.

I hoped she wasn't going to go off on one of her rants about how things were in her day. She was forever saying she'd loved this neighborhood when she was a kid, when there were always kids playing outside on the streets and people sitting on their stoops talking.

I stepped up to our front door and let the scanner read my face. I said my name and password while Mom lingered on the street.

These streets used to make me feel safe. And inside the foyer, the gleaming hardwood floors so shiny you could see your face in them and the historic-trust sage green walls with wide antique white molding—all of which Mom had painstakingly restored—used to make me feel safe, too. Now I wasn't so sure.

I ran upstairs, yelling that I had tons of homework to catch up on. Maybe I said I had an exam to study for. I don't really remember. I just remember collapsing on my bed, willing my body to sink deep into the cushiony recesses of the foam mattress, hoping it would swallow me whole. I stared at the white lace canopy over my antique bed. At the pale pink walls. At my yearbook clippings from freshman year—the blurbs I'd written about the new tennis coach and the boy most likely to conquer the corporate world—taped to the walls like so many leaves fluttering in the lazy breeze from the ceiling fan. I stared without really seeing anything until I heard voices downstairs.

Mom and Dad were talking, laughing easily with each other. I'd always loved that sound. It was like ice tinkling in a glass. And I knew that he'd probably given her flowers or her favorite bottle of wine. Dad has connections. That's what he always says. I also knew he'd be supersweet all evening, calling her Siddy. I knew this because that's what he did every time she came home from TFC. I just never put it all together. Why hadn't I?

I tried to study, but the words wouldn't sit still on the page.

Dad brought up dinner to my room later.

"Hi, Princess. Mom told me you have an exam tomorrow," he said, sliding the tray in front of me. He'd brought me tuna salad and diet soda. No cocoa.

"History," I said, pretending to be absorbed in the book. I wasn't even sure it was a history book.

"How was today?" He sounded genuinely interested. He sat down on the bed and waited.

I looked up at him. He'd changed into his usual khakis and golf shirt and the old flip-flops he wore around the house. His "beachcomber wear," he liked to call it. He looked like the same old Dad he'd always been. The same guy who'd told me fantastic bedtime stories about pirates when I was small. The same guy who'd sat up with me last year when both Mom and I had the flu. How could that guy do what Mom said he did? He looked at me so innocently and so full of Dadness that I began to doubt what I'd heard.

"Okay," I finally answered. "Kind of boring actually. A lot of waiting," I added, knowing he'd expect me to say something clueless and glossy like that.

Dad pulled something out of his pocket. A small, greenish blue box that I instantly recognized as being from the best jewelry store, the Tiffany's downtown next to his office. Inside was a silver bracelet with one charm on it. A purse. It was, I had to admit, very glossy.

He fastened it onto my wrist. I couldn't help smiling.

"No little girl of mine should have to see what you saw," he said, full of seriousness. "But the world isn't a safe place anymore, and I can't always be there to protect you. So every time you need to forget something bad like you did today, I'm going to buy you a new charm to remind you that you're still my little girl."

I did the only thing I could think to do. I hugged him.

With his arms around me, I breathed him in; his familiar scent—a dab of Father's Day cologne, a whiff of cigar, all mixed together with the smell of him—had always made me feel safe. But now it only confused me.

* * *

Later that evening, as I was feeding my untouched plate of food into the disposal, I heard Mom and Dad talking in the media room. They were watching that spy 'cast *Hearts and Minds* on the big screen. The hero always saves some village in the nick of time with only a wad of gum and a paper clip, winning the undying love of the locals and turning them against the Coalition. Dad loves that stuff.

"Oh, so now you're the security expert?"

"Keep your voice down, Ethan."

"So what if she hears? You can take her with you now."

* * *

That night the dream came again. The bones rattled. The ash rained down. The socks were bright red. But the air smelled of expensive cigars and cheap cologne.

Afterward I couldn't sleep. I lay in bed afraid of what I might see if I closed my eyes. When I did, I saw flashes of red and the look on Mom's ashen face in the cold, white room. I wished I'd taken that pill.

As I tossed and turned, I could feel the coolness of my new charm bracelet on the skin of my wrist. A silver purse was a great charm, very me, but something bugged me about it.

I crawled out of bed and scanned the ID chip in the bracelet with my mobile. Since the bracelet was a gift, the purchase price was blacked out, which I didn't care about. And I didn't care about the warranty or materials, either, so I touched general history and skimmed through the two paragraphs there.

Though charm bracelets go as far back as ancient Egypt, and charms themselves even farther, charm bracelets like the one I had were first big in the 1950s. It was all the rage to have charms to commemorate a girl's rites of passage. Sweet sixteen. Graduation. Wedding. Baby.

Now they were back in style, although jewelers had never stopped making them. And each charm was still some kind of a reminder of a key event in a girl's life. A memento, you might say. The entry ended with a cheesy ad of a dad giving a girl very much like me a new charm. *Remember*, the ad said. *Remember the milestones in her life*.

Apparently my milestone was an explosive shopping trip. Dad was more right than he knew.

5

I Need a New Word

Therapeutic Statement 42-03282028-11
Subject: *JAMES, NORA EMILY, 15*
Facility: *HAMILTON DETENTION CENTER TFC-42*

The next day I was showing off my new bracelet to my girls at my locker when I saw the kid with the cast lurking around the windows. I hadn't noticed it so much at the TFC, but he had that retro-skate-punk look down. It was so thirty-years-ago that it was almost cool again. Almost. My girls were all over me about the TFC experience and how many points I got for the first visit.

"I'm going to save my points, when I get some, for a shot at being an extra on *Behind the Gates*," one of my girls said.

I was putting on lip gloss when I noticed that the ad playing on my locker door was for Profile Body Spray for men. I hadn't picked it in my preferences, and I seriously doubted any of my girls had it in theirs.

"I hear you're not a virgin anymore," a guy said to me.

My girls went quiet as I turned to look at him. It was Tom Slayton, captain of the lacrosse team.

He tapped his temple and grinned. "Had my first experience last year."

The girls giggled and said they'd see me in yearbook as they disappeared into the crowded halls.

I managed a smile.

"The team is having a party this weekend at my place. Want to come? Your friends are invited, too."

Normally I'd have been thrilled. Sophomores never get invited to those parties. And Tom was tall and blond and overall easy on the eyes. But I could still see cast-boy sitting near the windows pretending not to watch me.

I nodded to Tom.

"Cool," he said.

The first bell rang. I told Tom I'd see him in Spanish.

I lingered by my locker, debating whether to say something to cast-boy. Finally I wandered over as casually as I could.

"Hey," I said. It came out a little squeakier than I intended.

"You remember me, huh?" he said, gathering up his olive-drab messenger bag with his good hand. "I'm honored." He didn't sound it.

I shrugged and checked the time on my mobile.

"You're not going to say anything about the pill, are you?" he asked, staring me down. Suddenly he didn't seem so sure of himself.

I shook my head. The second bell rang, and I started off in the direction of my biology class. Then, I'm not sure why, I turned back. "I didn't take it, either."

I'd never seen anyone's jaw literally drop open before.

The tardy bell rang. "Shit." I started to run toward bio.

I heard wheels drop to the linoleum behind me. Cast-boy rolled up beside me on his skateboard.

"We should talk. Meet me in the library after school," he said before he pushed off down the hall. "I'm Micah, by the way, Micah Wallenberg," he added over his shoulder, right before he almost crashed into Mr. Peters, my geometry teacher.

"Get off that board, young man," Mr. Peters said.

*　*　*

I debated all day about going to see Micah after school. He didn't exactly fit in with my group of friends. I wouldn't say there are cliques at Homeland Inc. Senior High. (Technically, we're Homeland High No. 17, one of the company's many schools in the Virginia-Maryland-DC area.) Obviously it's a free country and you can talk to whoever you want. But you are expected to hang out with the kids like you, the ones into the same things, going the same places. My crowd was into yearbook, student council, social clubs, and sports. We were going to Columbia and Stanford and Duke after we got out of here. Micah's crowd was into skateboarding and piercing their eyebrows. And I had no idea where they were headed.

I thought about all that as we discussed what events

to cover for this year's book. As I looked at my girls—my funny, glossy-headed girls—bubbling away about the prom (which was only a month away), the fund-raising drives, and class trips, I realized I could never talk to them about what I was supposed to have forgotten.

After yearbook I called the parentals to let them know I'd be home late.

* * *

Micah sat with his back to the art stacks, his cast propped up on a pile of coffee-table books. I could just see his curly brown head bent over something, his good hand working furiously with a pencil. As soon as I got close to the table, his head popped up and he smiled a quick, happy-to-see-you-showed-up grin. Then he pulled out the chair for me with his good arm. And I could see what he'd been doing. Sketching. Me.

It was a stylized comic-book exaggeration of me: skinnier and with actual boobs. My brown hair hung down over one green eye. My designer jeans were a little tighter. And I was poised to defend myself from the attack of a band of giant ninja pills.

"Not bad," I said. Actually, it was really good. "Did you do one of yourself?"

He flipped back a few pages. It was him, only more so. The curls were wilder and darker. The glasses were not as Harry Potterish. His goatee wasn't as penciled in. But he wore the same dark green T-shirt with a big black star on the front, not-too-baggy black jeans, and clown-sized skateboard kicks. In the picture, colored pencils spilled out of the green messenger bag that hung from his side; they were drawing an even more exaggerated caricature of him on the sidewalk.

He showed me a few other sketches. One was of a Japanese girl with pink spiky hair tinkering with a windmill made out of mannequin parts in a garden of equally crazy-looking sculptures or machines.

"My friend Winter Nomura," he said. "I met her in welding class." She went to our school, but I'd never really paid attention to the faces in his crowd.

Then he showed me a series of drawings, like panels of a comic strip, of his character getting pummeled under the bleachers by apes in football jerseys. The numbers on the jerseys gave away who they were supposed to be.

"That was the first memory I was supposed to have erased," he said. "At least that I remember." He flipped to the next page. "This one was my own damn fault."

The comic strip showed Micah skating through traffic downtown, a spray can in hand, and then getting hit by a big black van at the corner of Market and First.

He explained that the cop at the scene had convinced his mom that he'd be scarred for life if he didn't "forget" about this incident. "He probably thought my accident was related to the big bombing up the street."

"The bookstore one," I said, putting it together. "That's where I was. That's what I was supposed to forget, too."

Micah picked up his pencil. "Tell me about it."

I did, and it just sort of flowed out of me, much easier

than it had at the TFC. Micah sketched as he listened. I stopped when I got to the part about seeing him in the waiting room.

"You didn't really spit out the pill because of me, did you?" he asked. He stopped sketching, and I noticed how brown his eyes were.

"No," I said after a few seconds. "It was my mother's memory." That was too private to tell anyone, to even say out loud. "Let's just say she's earning her frequent-forgetting points. And somebody needed to remember that."

Micah looked at me as if I'd said the most profound thing on Earth. "Yeah, they do," he said finally. He gathered up his sketchbook and pencils, shoving them into his messenger bag with his good hand. Then he leaned over and kissed me on the cheek before grabbing the skateboard he'd stashed under his seat. I was too dumbstruck to say anything. He looked over his shoulder as he stood up.

"Same time Monday?" he asked.

I nodded.

I waited until he left to look around to see if anyone had noticed us. Micah wasn't really date material, not in my crowd, but I couldn't help feeling pretty glossy.

Maybe I needed a new word.

6

The Hummingbirds Awaken

Therapeutic Statement *42-03282028-13*
Subject: *NOMURA, WINTER, 14*
Facility: *HAMILTON DETENTION CENTER TFC-42*

The hummingbirds had been slumbering peacefully in my brain until that day. Velvet tagged along with me to get a book on Jean Tinguely's work that I had reserved at the library. He created these amazing abstract metal machines that showed how ridiculous everything was.

"Why don't you just download this shit?" Velvet whispered as we walked up to the front desk. I didn't answer her. I had tried to explain before that I liked to touch the pictures. The real sculptures would've been even better. But the thing with my parents meant I'd never get an exit visa to go see Tinguely's work in person. It was all in Switzerland and France.

Ms. Curtis smiled tightly at us as she handed me two books. I don't think she knew what to make of my crowd.

Velvet could construct a runway-worthy ensemble out of a trash bag and a shoelace—and look darn good in it. Our other friends dressed like the rock stars and *artistes* they thought they were. My only outward expression of inner nonconformity was my hair. It was pink that day.

"I thought you might like this one, too," Ms. Curtis said, tapping the second book.

The top book was the one I'd ordered; the other was about Alexander Calder. He sculpted mobiles and painted airplanes.

I took the Calder book. It had a striking red mobile on the cover. Maybe I could make a sculpture driven by the sun, like solar chimes, and they could play something really annoying.

I looked up. Ms. Curtis had said something that evidently required an answer on my part. I nodded. She continued talking about her trip to the National Gallery over Christmas break with a guy who didn't appreciate art. He *was* into music, though, she added, as if that made him acceptable in my eyes. Ms. Curtis, with her cute blonde bob, perfect complexion, and matching sweater set, might not *get* us; but maybe she wanted to *be* us—just a little.

Velvet nudged me. "That can only end badly," she said as she nodded in the direction of the table by the art stacks.

My best friend, Micah, and a girl, both with their heads down, almost touching, were working away at something. They were totally absorbed in whatever they were doing—and each other. It was as if they were in their own private bubble.

And the girl was Nora James.

Velvet was so right—for so many reasons. This was going to be bad. In my head, the whirring noise, like the running in my dreams, like the beating of hummingbird wings, returned. With a vengeance. Shit. I mumbled a good-bye, grabbed my books, and exited the library, Velvet hot on my heels.

"I thought you guys were just friends," she said.

"That isn't it." And she knew it. She knew I was obsessed with someone else.

Velvet put her arm around me. "Why don't we try some retail therapy? Thrift shop variety, of course. Cheap but still therapeutic. Or we could dye our hair blue."

Velvet smelled like lavender. And she did look like Jet. The hummingbirds settled down to a dull flutter.

I chose the blue option.

7

Minus the Gates

Therapeutic Statement *42-03282028-11*
Subject: *JAMES, NORA EMILY, 15*
Facility: *HAMILTON DETENTION CENTER TFC-42*

That evening Dad's car service took the girls and me to the football game and the lacrosse team party after it. I won't bore you with party details—those are memories I want to keep, anyway—but let's just say I doubted Micah would have fit in very well. I told myself as the service dropped me off that I wasn't going to see him again.

And I kept thinking that all weekend.

Then Sunday evening we had a rare occurrence in our house: we all ate dinner together. We are like one of the *Behind the Gates* families, minus the gates. Everyone is successful. Busy. Off doing their own thing. Dad, aka Ethan Trevor James III, is a partner in Soft Target Security; and he runs some sort of operations center downtown for his biggest customer, TFC. I'd never been beyond the lobby because of the restrictions, but I imagined the people inside staring at banks and banks of monitors, watching every TFC in the world for break-ins or whatever. When he's not working, which he always is, Dad likes to play golf or have drinks with his clients. They usually live in swanky compounds or high-rise security complexes.

Mom—Sidney Woolf James—who I've probably made sound like a shopaholic, is a real estate attorney. She used to practice some other type of law when I was little, but now she handles the legal stuff on the sale of the pricey houses and lofts that Dad's clients live in. I think it bores her. She rarely talks about it except to mention something about the house, like it's a Craftsman bungalow or it used to be a shoe factory back in the day. She likes places with character and history. Places that don't all look the same, she says. Places where you can see the lives that came before you. We always go on a celebratory shopping spree after a juicy closing.

So I naturally tuned into the conversation when Mom mentioned she had a closing tomorrow afternoon for a property in Los Palamos. It's one of those *Behind the Gates* compounds with its own schools, malls, and even police force. You never really need to leave. And you don't have to worry about the city curfew as long as you stay in the compound.

Mom winked at me. I knew she was thinking major shopping trip. Usually that would've thrilled me, but this time it made me feel queasy and hot.

"I have a lot of clients at Los Palamos," Dad said. "Great golf course. Brand-new mall. Excellent schools."

"Zero privacy. Twenty-four/seven surveillance," Mom answered. "And they're using that chip that lets them know where you are all the time." Mom obviously didn't think this was a good thing. "You can't turn it off."

"Not one car bomb since it opened," Dad said, looking at me. "Nora, you'd like to live there, wouldn't you?"

"It does sound nice," I answered carefully, looking from Mom to Dad. "But I'd hate to change schools right now." It was true. I had another two months left of my sophomore year at Homeland. And there was the prom and the yearbook.

Of course, I was also thinking a move might solve a lot of problems. Micah would be zero temptation there. Maybe the bad dreams would go away. Maybe we would be safer, but I wasn't sure I could trust Dad anymore.

"You'll make great friends there, the right ones," Dad said as if it were already settled. He turned back to Mom. "There's a house coming on the market today. The guy's getting transferred to L.A. You'll both love it."

"Don't those places have waiting lists?" I asked. One of my friends had moved to a compound last year. Her folks had put their names on the list when she first started school.

"You didn't, did you?" Mom asked, glaring at Dad. "You put us on the damn list without asking me. Knowing how I felt. When were you planning on telling me?"

"When we got to the top of the list." Dad grinned. "Now."

Mom didn't say anything.

"So we're moving?" I asked.

"Yes, Princess, on the first," he said. That was less than a month away.

Dad described the house. Lots of space. A pool in the backyard. A panic room in the basement. My own bathroom. And maybe next year I could even have my own car, he said, only to be driven within the compound. The insurance was so much cheaper inside the gates, he explained.

He did make it sound pretty glossy. He tried to placate Mom with the promise of a double commission. She was furious, though. And something else. That measuring, all-there look in her eyes reminded me of something I hadn't seen in a long time. It reminded me of mornings years ago when she'd get ready for court by practicing her remarks on me as I ate my Cheerios. I'd forgotten about that woman. That woman had been fierce.

"We would've gotten a house there years ago if it hadn't been for your mother's 'past,'" he said, his grin colder and thinner.

"Ethan," Mom said sharply. But her tone didn't stop him.

"And then maybe Nora would never have seen what she saw, never even come close to something like that, just to go shopping." He spat out the last word, but he looked especially pleased with himself. And with that, the other woman, that other Mom was gone.

She stared at her plate. He cut into his meat and stabbed a chunk of it into his mouth, clearly enjoying it. The red of the nearly rare meat turned my stomach. I concentrated on my peas, not sure what to make of the situation. Or my new insight into it. How did I not notice all this tension before? Maybe I did but just didn't take it seriously. Now I could see this tug-of-war going on between them, and it was weighted against her. And the more she lost, the more he held it against her.

For a few minutes all I heard was the sound of chewing. I closed my eyes, and all I saw was red. And the word *memento*. That's when I decided.

"Uh, I need to stay after school tomorrow to work on a project," I said without looking up from my plate. "Art history."

Dad said he'd send a car to pick me up. In fact, he'd send my own driver to pick me up every day until we moved, he added. Then he hurried out the door, muttering about meeting a client for drinks.

*   *   *

The next morning as I picked at my oatmeal, Dad sailed down the stairs. He pecked me on the cheek and slid a brand-new Nomura Pink Ice mobile, all pearly and paper-thin, across the countertop to me.

"It's all set up for you, Princess. ID. Allowance. School-work. And just press one for the car service," he told me. He leaned over toward Mom. She turned to avoid his kiss. He grabbed her toast and headed out the door.

After breakfast I caught her dabbing makeup on her right cheekbone, and I knew where she'd be going before her closing this afternoon.

And I knew where I'd be.

8

Free Speech and
All That

Therapeutic Statement 42-03282028-11
Subject: JAMES, NORA EMILY, 15
Facility: HAMILTON DETENTION CENTER TFC-42

Micah sat in the same spot near the art section, hunched over his sketch pad, a stack of books blocking what he was drawing.

"I didn't think you were coming," he said, peeking over the books.

"Me neither." I wondered if they were the same books that had been there Friday.

He pulled out my chair for me again and then slid his sketch pad in front of me. My story was all there. Almost. The comic was eight boxes, or what he called "panels," stacked in tiers on a regular sheet of paper. The first panel, the biggest one, showed a body splatting to the pavement at my feet. The next showed me waking up in a sweat. The graffiti. TFC. Him with his cast. Spitting out the pill. It was all there. The fat black pen strokes pinned the action to the crisp white page. It was in black and white, no color at all, but it seemed realer, not so cartoony that way. He hadn't put the words in yet, but the action told the story. It was odd, like seeing myself from a distance. Not a bad odd, though. It was as if I were far enough away to see the whole story and not get hung up on a scene.

"You said someone needs to remember," he said. "I was thinking maybe we could do it with a comic book. Okay, more like a comic strip. With our stories. And maybe other kids could tell us their memories before they get erased."

I didn't look up at him, although I could feel how close he was and how much he wanted to do this. I stared at the section of the comic where I was in the treatment room. Micah didn't include Mom's memory because I hadn't told him what it was. In the frame, I just hid the pill under my tongue. (I spit it out in the last frame.) But something wasn't quite right.

"Do you ever dream about getting beat up or the van hitting you?" I asked him, but I was really thinking about the comic strip.

"Yeah." He shrugged. "My dreams aren't as bad as they used to be. Drawing helps, I think."

"It doesn't make sense."

He looked confused, and I couldn't blame him. My brain doesn't always follow a straight line.

"What I did." I pointed to the treatment room panel. "It doesn't make sense—as a story—unless you know what my mother's memory was."

He nodded thoughtfully. Then I told him. And I told him she was probably there at the TFC now.

Micah looked like someone had punched him in the gut. It was actually kind of sweet.

"Wow." He let out a long breath and touched my hand.

Then he ripped off a clean sheet of paper and handed me a pencil.

"You write. I'll draw," he said firmly.

We sat there, quiet, our heads together, our pencils moving across paper as if we were channeling something, until my mobile buzzed to tell me the car service was outside waiting for me.

"What are we going to call this?" he asked as I helped him stuff everything into his bag. He banged his bum arm against the table in the process.

I tapped his cast and turned to leave. "*Memento*, of course," I said over my shoulder. He wasn't the only one who could make an exit.

I didn't have the dream that night.

* * *

Later that week, after we had a solid first draft together, it occurred to us that we might need to disguise ourselves. I didn't want my friends or family to figure out it was me. He was sure SWAT teams and black helicopters would drag us away if we didn't cover our tracks.

We talked about several ways to do this. He even tried making our characters into animals. I thought it would be too cutesy until he showed me this old graphic novel about the Holocaust, where the Jews were mice and the

Nazis were pigs. It definitely wasn't cute. Micah tried using sheep and wolves for our people, but he gave up on that idea because they kept coming out too Disney. So we stuck with people. He came up with different characters. We changed the names, tweaked the story lines a little. The whole protect-the-innocent thing, especially since the innocent was us.

Then we realized something else. We didn't know how to produce or distribute *Memento* without getting caught. I didn't think it was a big deal. Free speech and all that. We should just upload it, I told him, and send it to everyone at school.

Micah laughed so hard when I said it that Ms. Curtis suggested it was time for us to go home.

"I know just the person who can help us," Micah whispered as he shoved his sketch pad into his bag. "Tell your car service you need to go to the downtown library tomorrow. I'll meet you there, and we'll go to my friend's place together. Okay?"

"Downtown?" I dreaded the thought of going down there again.

"Don't worry," Micah said. "I have your back."

And I knew he did.

9

Nothing Works Anymore

Therapeutic Statement 42-03282028-13
Subject: NOMURA, WINTER, 14
Facility: HAMILTON DETENTION CENTER TFC-42

One of the hands, the one with the silver watch painted on the wrist, flopped to the ground like a dead fish. No matter how tight I ratcheted the hands to the armature, one would eventually work its way off. I threw the hand across the garden, smacking it into the bamboo gate—just as Sasuke-san walked through in his best blue suit. His only suit really. He only wore it to one place, and he looked so tired and old and small in it today.

"Ay, Win-chan," he said. "Watch it." He was annoyed, but not at me.

"Sorry, Grandfather," I said. "I can't get this stupid sculpture to work right." Then I launched into a tirade about kinetic sculptures, school, and what an idiot Micah was. I don't know what I said. I was just babbling to distract my grandfather. And myself. Anything to keep us from talking about *it*.

"We'll talk later," he said. I knew without him saying it anyway. The motion didn't work. Another lawyer quit. We didn't get visitation rights. Again.

Nothing worked right anymore.

"I'm going to change," my grandfather said as he picked up the hand and tossed it to me.

"Micah's coming over later," I told him. "He's bringing a girl. Nora James."

Sasuke-san raised an eyebrow. I shook my head. Sure, I liked Micah, but more like a brother. The idiot brother you have to look out for. And maybe this girl wasn't the best thing for my idiot brother, but that's not what was bugging me about her. At the moment.

"Who was Mom and Dad's first lawyer?" I asked. "That lady you liked."

"Sidney James," he said slowly and more like a question. "Oh," he said silently, and walked back to the house.

I turned the mannequin hand over in mine. Maybe if I added some weight to the hand, maybe a real wrist watch, it would balance out all of the hands, keep them turning like gears. And maybe if I added solar cells and mobile processors to those sheets of canvas I'd found, it would drown out the sounds I hear in my head whenever I slow down long enough to listen.

10

Whatever That Is

Therapeutic Statement 42-03282028-11
Subject: JAMES, NORA EMILY, 15
Facility: HAMILTON DETENTION CENTER TFC-42

From the downtown library Micah and I walked to the corner
of Eighth and Day. The edge of the warehouse district. Mom
had said once that this area used to be nice. Trendy lofts.
High-priced condos. Hip clubs. It wasn't so trendy now.
Most of the buildings were boarded up. A bombed-out car,
the rust thick on its body like scales, hugged the curb at
Sixth and Day. The air smelled of rotting garbage.

I stayed close to Micah as I followed him down an alley
to a chain-link fence covered with faded Nomura Electron-
ics signs. Between the boards, all you could see was metal.
Micah pushed on a sign, and it slid open like a patio door,
revealing a hole in the chain-link fence.

Once inside the fence I was eyeball to eyeball with a
forest of steel poles and wooden beams. My first impression

was that we were under the bleachers, as if there were some secret stadium here. Turns out there was.

"What is this place?" I demanded.

"You'll see it better once we get out from under the seats."

We walked along under the back row until we emerged into the open. There I saw a giant playground of steel, rope, and Plexiglas. It looked as if it had been built from those metal building sets Dad bought me when I was little and then played with all Christmas Day by himself.

Micah jumped on the bleachers and bounded up to the top. "From here you can see the whole layout."

With a groan, I followed him up there. I took in the crazy quilt of structures. A log with handholds carved out of it hanging over a partially filled pond. A big fish net flapping over a dry pond. A canyon of clear walls.

"It's an obstacle course," I concluded.

"Yeah, Winter's granddad lets me skateboard on that one." Micah pointed to a curved wall that looked like a massive wave. It had to have been twenty feet high.

"He built this whole thing years ago to practice for some goofy Japanese game show," Micah added.

"Uh, cool." It wasn't.

"Oh, this isn't the cool part," Micah said, beaming. "Over there, behind the Spider Climb." He pointed to a tower of scaffolding at the far end of the yard.

"Don't they have security?" I asked. We hadn't needed a retina or voice scan or even a key code to get this far.

Micah shrugged. "They have some sort of system on the house itself. Winter leaves the back 'gate' open so I can skate or hang out whenever."

As we cut across the course, I noticed that some of the obstacles were missing pieces. Some of the rope was frayed and rotting. Boards were missing.

The Spider Climb turned out to be two walls of slippery Plexiglas you evidently had to climb to get to a rope, which you then had to shinny up about thirty feet to reach a buzzer on the top.

Just beyond the tower there was a bamboo gate. It opened into a whole different world. I don't know what I was expecting after the adult jungle gym we'd just passed through. Definitely not this.

"This is Winter's garden," Micah announced as we stepped into it. And I had to admit it. This *was* the cool part.

A bamboo wall encircled a crisscross of polished wooden paths and white sand. It was almost peaceful, like something out of a Japanese home-and-garden show. Or a martial arts movie. Almost. Except that instead of bonsai trees and big rocks planted in the sand, there were these eerie metal sculptures. And they moved. At least the first one did.

Though it was just a few big twists of burnished metal, it looked like a hunched-over man pawing at a pool of water. His hands slapped at the surface of the water, sending out bigger and bigger ripples.

"Watch this," Micah whispered, pointing to the next thing in the garden. It looked like a metal shopping bag lying on its side.

The water started to lap up onto the sand by the bag. Two slender black pieces of metal peeked out of the bag and felt their way to the ground. The feelers or legs crab walked themselves partially out of the bag, and the creature started to pull itself, bag and all, up the sloped walk. Its frenzied back-and-forth motion reminded me of something.

"Are those windshield wipers?" I asked, thoroughly impressed—and unnerved.

He nodded, a big grin on his face.

Something about the jerky, almost desperate crawl of the wipers dragging the shopping bag shell behind them made me uneasy. Then as the whole thing reached the top of its little hill, it stopped crawling, collapsed back into its shell, and slid back down to where it had started. It was like it couldn't get anywhere with that bag on its back.

The next thing—a windmill of metal hands beating at the air—started moving. The flailing motion of the hands as they reached the top of the windmill and then started back down reminded me of someone drowning. A limb fell off into the sand. The spiky-haired girl from Micah's drawing scooped up the creature's hand and then clicked a button on a remote control. The creature shuddered to a stop.

Winter Nomura bounded up the walkway to meet us. I could imagine her skinny arms and legs spider walking her way up the Plexiglas tower we'd just passed through.

"I'm going to have to redo the servo mechanism on that

one," she said quietly, almost as if she didn't want it to hear.

"That shopping bag crab is still the glossiest thing you've ever made," Micah said.

She cringed.

"That thing is *so* not glossy," I said. I blurted it out before I really thought about it. I didn't mean to insult her work. I meant the opposite.

Winter peered at me as if she'd just noticed Micah wasn't alone.

She looked exactly like he'd drawn her, except that her hair was now blue. She had an intensity that was hard to capture on paper. Very quiet, yet if you shook her up, she'd explode like a bottle of soda. Her almost black eyes bore through me as if she had X-ray vision and could see exactly how I worked. She was more unnerving than her creatures.

"It's not supposed to be," she said after what seemed like an eternity. "Glossy, that is." She turned off that X-ray vision and almost smiled. Almost. I felt like I'd passed some test.

Micah didn't seem to notice. Or maybe he was used to Winter by now. He was babbling on about this project of ours and how we needed her help. We let him babble.

"Your garden is beautiful," I said, adding, "in an eerie sort of way. It's—unsettling."

"That it's supposed to be," she said. And this time she did smile.

She showed us the other sculptures she was working on—"kinetic" sculptures she called them. The last one was just a pile of canvas and wires and circuits so far.

"I have this idea," she said, excited, "to do something with solar sails. Not sure exactly what yet." She led us to the pagoda in the center of her garden. There she'd laid out dozens of tiny solar cells on a low table. She'd also cracked open several old mobiles and other electronica and was creating something on a circuit board. "I think the sails will be like chimes, the sunlight powering ring tones or something crazy like that. Maybe car alarms."

I picked up a mobile she'd gutted. "I thought you weren't supposed to open these," I said. There was clearly a warning sticker on the back: under penalty of law blah-blah-blah.

"If you can't open it . . . ," she began.

"You don't really own it," Micah finished for her as if he'd heard it a million times.

"Anyway," she said, "I'm going to put one final piece in here." She pointed to the table. "Don't know yet what it'll be, but it'll run off the solar panels on the roof. And it'll kind of sum up everything." She shrugged. "Whatever that is."

A gate on the other side of the garden creaked open. A wiry older man, dressed in track pants, a T-shirt, and a black hat like you see in old black-and-white movies, brought out a tray.

"Win-chan, tea for your guests." He set out cups and a teapot on the table. "Two sugars for you, Micah." Micah bowed his head slightly. "One for you?" he asked, looking at me, scrutinizing my sugar intake, I guess. I nodded.

"And a triple shot of espresso for my little whirlwind." The liquid in the cup he handed Winter was as black as ink. "Six sugars," he added with a grimace.

"I'm Koji Yamada, Winter's grandfather," he said, putting the tray aside to extend his hand to me.

"Nora James," I introduced myself. I couldn't help staring at his arm. Both arms. They were covered in designs. A snake flowed down his right arm with the head ending at his hand. A tiger pounced down his left arm in full color.

"Those are beautiful. How long do they last?" I asked.

"Forever," Mr. Yamada answered, amused.

"They're real tattoos," Winter said. "You know, needles stabbing ink into your flesh."

"Why?" I asked, blurting out again. Something about these people, or maybe their art, gave me the blurts. No one got real tattoos anymore. "What if you get tired of them?" I asked.

"Each of my tats means something to me." He pointed to a cherry blossom on the left side of his neck. "Birth of my child." He pulled down the top of his T-shirt to reveal a snowflake over his heart. "My grandchild." He pointed to some Japanese writing on his right wrist. "My first shop." The snake. "Knowledge." The tiger. "Protection.

"Why would I want to change those? They're the things that make me who I am." Then he added, "Besides, would you buy clothes from a naked man?"

I didn't want that picture in my head, particularly if that man had tattoos.

"Grandfather owns a chain of tattoo shops," Winter explained in that same hushed tone she'd used when talking about her creations.

"I'll leave you kids alone." Mr. Yamada headed toward the back garden gate, the one we'd come through, stopping to stretch his calves on the walkway.

"Sasuke-san," Winter called after him. "I sort of borrowed some stuff from the Curtain Cling." She gestured toward the pile of canvas.

"Like the curtains, huh?" He sighed. "I was never any good at that one, anyway." He disappeared through the gate.

• • •

We showed Winter our first comic. Micah spread it out on the table for her to read. I couldn't help rereading it alongside her, and it filled me with an odd sense of pride and rightness. We really had something here.

Winter said nothing as she read. When she finished, she took an agonizingly long sip of her thick, jet-black espresso.

"I see your problem," she finally said.

Micah nodded.

"I don't," I said. "I still say upload it. Who's going to care if we send this to a few dozen kids—or the whole world, for that matter? It's a free country."

"Tell that to my parents," Winter said. She collected our teacups and carefully stacked them on the tray. I wasn't finished with mine.

"Look, Winnie-chan," Micah said. He got up and took the tray.

"Don't call me Winnie," she snapped as she opened the gate into the house.

I had heard the softness in his voice and something in hers that made me wonder about their relationship. I felt a little jealous. Kind of like a third wheel. The preppie girl among artists. It didn't help when they came back out laughing.

* * *

"You need two things really," Winter said. Her irritation had evaporated. "A way to produce. And a way to distribute. I can help with the first one."

Her eye twitched slightly, as if it couldn't take all the energy or caffeine coursing through her spidery body.

"Okay. Now all computers—mobiles, home, school, work—are part of one big network."

"One monitored network," Micah interjected.

"Exactly," Winter agreed. "Ditto the printers, copiers, TVs, cars, refrigerators, etcetera. All of them are dumb devices that pull everything—programs, files, information—from a central server. No memory of their own.

"You could upload and distribute *Memento* with your mobile or your bedroom computer, but the government—and the handful of security corporations that run it—will know exactly who you are, and they could block the file. Even if you just jury-rigged a stand-alone printer and handed out the comic books in the bathrooms at school, they could still trace the nanomarkers in the ink."

"Central control of the information," Micah said, tapping his temple.

"But who's going to care? We have the right to say what we want," I argued.

"My parents thought so," Winter said. "Grandfather's lawyer says they're still alive, but she hasn't been able to see them for over a year. And neither have we. The first lawyer gave up on the case."

She looked at me with that X-ray vision of hers again; but I was a blank, as blank as when Mr. Peters tried to explain tangents. I felt the rays bounce off of me.

"They're in Detention," Micah said. "With a big *D*. You know the place they hold people for 'questioning' and ultimately the Big Pill that makes them forget everything."

"There's no such place." Dad's in security, I told myself. He would've mentioned such a thing. It would have been on the news. We would have learned about it in school. I looked from Micah to Winter, hoping this was some big joke. No one was laughing. "They can't just hold people. Or make them take the pill."

"Can't they?" Winter stood up. "Your mother was their first lawyer. Ask her about it."

"Winter?" Micah said. He seemed just as surprised as I was.

"No way," I said.

"She lasted the longest. A year."

"What did your parents do?" I asked her.

She shrugged. "Nothing. My folks were engineers. Mom

designed microchips; Dad created software for his family's firm."

Of course, *that* Nomura. I felt the outline of the Nomura Pink Ice in the pocket of my new leather jacket.

I figured it couldn't hurt to be careful. Still, I thought, the Nomuras must have done something wrong. Maybe I would ask Mom, though I seriously doubted she'd know anything about it.

"Okay, so how do we print this thing?" I asked after a moment.

"Oh, I'll come up with something." Winter looked around the garden. "People printed underground comics long before computers."

*   *   *

"She's full of crap about my mom, right?" I asked Micah as we walked through the obstacle course on our way back to the library.

"Beats me," he said. "Watch this." He pointed to Mr. Yamada standing at the lip of the giant curved wall.

"Sasuke—the guy the game show was named after—was this ninja warrior in Japanese comic books and kids' stories," Micah explained.

Mr. Yamada pushed off the lower part of the wall and, with a couple of long, quick strides, propelled himself up the curve, then grabbed the overhanging lip of the wall. He pulled himself up in one fluid motion.

"He was raised by monkeys," Micah said as if that explained everything. "The ninja, not Mr. Yamada," he added when he saw the confused look on my face.

Mr. Yamada stood on the giant concrete wave shaking out his arms, looking out over the world, the city, as if he were taking in one last look before the wave crashed down and wiped it all away. Only then did he notice us. Micah bowed, and I did the same. Mr. Yamada nodded to us ever so slightly before he turned and leaped over the chasm to the next obstacle, disappearing from view.

And I'd thought *sasuke-san* was Japanese for "grandfather."

11

Not My Usual Glossy Self

Therapeutic Statement 42-03282028-11
Subject: JAMES, NORA EMILY, 15
Facility: HAMILTON DETENTION CENTER TFC-42

Mom and I finally fit in our post-closing shopping trip on Saturday. I'd been putting it off, using this "art history" project with Micah as an excuse. But really, the idea of shopping, especially downtown, was just too dreary for me.

So Mom had the car service take us to the Valley Ridge Mall. It's not the glossiest place, but it's okay. They don't require an identity chip to shop. Mom would probably rather see me get a tattoo than an ID chip, although we'll both need one to live in Los Palamos.

"These shoes would look cute on you," Mom said, pointing out a pair of these aqua blue Mary Jane sneakers with gel soles in the window of Shoe City.

I shrugged. They were cute, but I already had something similar in my closet. In pink.

"Or maybe you need something a little older." Mom pointed to a pair of red leather flats on the display table.

I wanted them less than the sneakers.

"Honey, are you okay?" Mom asked. "You don't seem your usual glossy self."

I looked at my mother—past her cute, short, cropped brown hair; her flawless makeup; her impeccable Georgia Tatum clothes—and saw this tiredness, this sadness in her hazel eyes that made me want to cry. It made me want to tell her everything, but I wasn't sure where to begin.

So I said I was fine.

She said we needed cookies. Big ones.

I used some of my TFC points to get us two huge chocolate chips and two small mochaccinos. Mom wanted to use hers, but I had five hundred points to burn and not a clue what I wanted to use them for. We sat in the food court of that cheesy mall and stared at our food for a couple of minutes.

"It's the move, isn't it?" she asked.

"I don't know," I answered. I actually hadn't thought much about moving to Los Palamos, but it was like three weeks away now. Mom had already started packing our winter clothes and the stuff in the basement.

"It'll be okay," she said, taking a tentative sip of her coffee. "Though it's certainly not my top choice of places to live." She took a big bite of her cookie.

"Why not?" I asked. But I really wanted to ask her something else.

"Locking people out—or in—isn't my idea of community,"

she said. "Back when our house was built, people sat out on their stoops and talked to one another. They knew one another. They didn't hide behind elaborate security systems and blast-proof windows. There was no curfew at night. You could walk or ride your bike or skateboard everywhere."

That was her rant about our neighborhood. Usually I tuned it out. Dad was always saying she lived in the past.

But this time I was listening.

She swished the whipped cream around in her coffee as she pondered something. "Moving to a compound just seems like giving in," she said after a few moments. "And I've done too much of that already."

I wasn't sure to what exactly she was giving in. Dad? Work? Life? Whatever it was, it looked like it was wearing her down.

"What did Dad mean about not getting a house there sooner?" I asked. He'd made it seem as if it was her fault they wouldn't let us in until now.

She sighed. "I don't know if you remember, but I used to practice a different kind of law. I had my own small firm—and I defended those people your father considers 'security risks.'"

I'd heard Dad talking about those quote-unquote people many times. That was *his* rant. He said real Americans worked hard and bought stuff for their families so that other real Americans could do the same thing. One gear turning the other, making the economic engine work, he liked to say. Anything else, anything that interfered with that, was un-American. Bad for business. Bad for the country. Good for the Coalition terrorists.

I usually ignored his rants, too.

"Ethan complained that it was hurting his business," Mom said. "And the law kept changing to make it nearly impossible for me to do my job. So I went into real estate."

I remembered when she'd switched. It was right after that trip to the beach. I was about six or seven, and Mom had gotten me out of bed one night. She'd packed our bags and said we were going on vacation. "Dad has to work," she'd said, "and we're leaving now so we can be there to see the sun rise over the ocean."

We'd stayed at a little cabin a block from the beach. The sheets smelled funky, and it had been cold out, too cold to swim. We'd walked barefoot on the rocky beach, eaten popcorn shrimp and saltwater taffy, and watched the stars at night. The beach town didn't have a curfew like Hamilton and the other big cities did. I'd loved that freedom. The world seemed so much bigger.

Then one evening just before sunset, as Mom and I hunted for sea beans along the shore, I saw a familiar figure walking toward us.

"Nora," Dad called. He was wearing jeans and flip-flops and a golf shirt under his Windbreaker.

I ran to him, but Mom didn't budge from her spot on the sand.

"I've missed you, Princess," he said as he wrapped me up in his jacket. It was warm and smelled like him. He gently steered me toward his car waiting by the road. "Ready to go home?" I turned back toward Mom, who was still standing there staring at us. "Mommy can bring your things when she comes. She has a new job starting soon," he said loud enough for her to hear.

Mom had come home at the end of the week.

I had to ask it now.

"Mom, were the Nomuras your clients, you know, before you switched?" I looked at her as if I were Winter watching one of her creations through those X-ray eyes, trying to see where it had gone wrong.

Mom looked at me blankly. "I don't think so, but my memory of clients from those days is a little hazy."

Then I remembered. The day after she'd come home from the beach, Mom had made her first trip to TFC.

The mall was beginning to close in around me. I needed some air.

"Can we get out of here?" I asked, not really waiting for her to answer as I threw away my cookie and half-filled cup of caffeinated crap.

We didn't buy anything else that day.

12

I Hate Pudding

Therapeutic Statement *42-03282028-13*
Subject: *NOMURA, WINTER, 14*
Facility: *HAMILTON DETENTION CENTER TFC-42*

I was in this room. It's the basement of our old house. Mom's treadmill was there. So was Dad's stinky futon from college that our old dog liked to sleep on. And my programmable Legos were scattered all over the floor. It smelled damp. Mom was running on the treadmill, a murder mystery cranked up on her earbuds. All I could hear were her sneakers beating out the time against the cranky whir of the treadmill belt. *Step. Whir. Step. Whir.*

Then there was banging upstairs. Men yelling. Mom kept running in place. *Step. Whir. Step. Whir.*

I ran into the next room, expecting to find the stairs. It was a closet. I backed out of it into the garage. I opened the door to the backyard, and I was in the attic. Then the guest room. The kitchen. I ran through rooms I didn't know we had. All the time I could hear her steps, steady like an old-fashioned clock.

Step. Whir. Step. Whir.

And everything smelled musty. The walls closed in on me, and I ran faster through room after room, calling for Mom and Dad in Japanese. A language I never learned.

Step. Whir. Step. Whir.

The sound grew louder, but I was no closer to getting back to her. Or anywhere familiar.

Then my grandfather ran past me and opened a door. It led into a big, white, empty room. He took me by the hand to the center. Then he bowed and disappeared. It was so quiet there, and there were no other doors or rooms; but I could still hear the sound of my mother running in my head. Running and going nowhere. The sound got louder, and I had no place else to go.

I always woke up at that point. Well, 99 percent of the time. Sometimes I dreamed I was filling up the white room with junk. But most of the time I'd wake up, fix a triple espresso, and then go out to my garden or workshop and tinker with my toys.

I know; my shrink told me I'm filling up that big white room in my soul with my creations, always moving, always making sounds to drown out that *step-whir* in my head. Duh. She wanted me to forget. Or at least to take the chill pills.

But who am I if I'm not that crazy artist girl?

No, if I take the chill pills, I'll feel like my brain is swimming in pudding. I won't see things clearly. I won't think at the speed of light. Sure, the meds will quiet the hummingbirds; but then my ideas won't buzz around in my head as if they had tiny wings, too.

A hummingbird would be a great tattoo. Grandfather won't let me get one until I'm eighteen, though. He said he promised Mom long ago.

Anyway, I decided to work on the tattoo machine I'm modding for Jet, Sasuke-san's best artist in his downtown shop. She's into real old-school Japanese tats, like koi fish and big back pieces with lots of color. She always dresses in old, turn-of-last-century-style clothes, but like adapted to today—and with a lot of leather—which might look stupid on some people. It looks hot on her.

So I was modifying this tattoo machine—the gunlike thing that pushes the ink into the skin—to look as if it stepped out of the pages of Jules Verne. I used pieces of copper, distressed wood, and a few gratuitous gears here and there to make it look Victorian. I threw some analog dials and gauges on the power supply to complete the effect.

I've done some similar mods for Jet's friends and mine. I've added copper pipe and an antique weather dial to Richie's bass. And I've etched a few mobiles to look like scrimshaw—you know, those designs sailors scratched out on whale bones and teeth hundreds of years ago. I've also made a few keyboards look like old metal typewriters, the ones with the round keys. Jet's friends call the style steam-punk, which was this literary-pop art style about thirty or forty years ago. It's all about making today's technology look like it would if it had been invented hundreds of years ago. I don't really see the point, but it's something to do in the wee hours of the morning when I'm too brain-dead to work on my own stuff.

I like things to be what they're going to be. Not what they were. Or could have been.

So, I finished the mod and wanted to test it out. It wasn't any good if Jet couldn't use it. I slipped an ink cartridge into the machine and tatted on the fleshy part of my left hand, between the thumb and the index finger. It stung as the needle jabbed into my skin. But it wasn't bad. Actually, I kind of got into it. The pain focused me. I just did a simple circle. Sort of calligraphy style, like I'd done it with a brush and not quite closed it.

The tattoo was red and bleeding when I got done; I cleaned it off and bandaged it. It would heal in a day or so. When I was done admiring my work, I noticed that it was already 8:30. I'd be late for school, if I went. So I decided I'd just go to Grandfather's shop to see Jet.

It doesn't open until ten; but she's always there early, cleaning, setting up her station, doing the books, etc.

*   *   *

"Damn, girl. That's so glossy," she said as I set down the machine on her table. She was wearing this leather corset thing and jeans. Like I said, she looked hot.

I dutifully groaned. It was a game we played. She knew I hated that word. She grinned.

"Seriously, Winter," she said. "That is the coolest mod you've done yet. Almost as cool as your sculptures."

"Sculptures?" a female voice asked from behind the dressing screen in the corner. I hadn't realized Jet had a customer. A woman emerged with a sheet clutched to her chest. She still had on dress pants and heels. Her hair and makeup were sleek and polished. Very corporate. She looked vaguely familiar, like I'd seen her on a 'cast; but I hardly ever watched except for the news. And the news was mostly mind-numbingly irrelevant, corporate-owned crap.

"She does kinetic sculptures. Very nonglossy," Jet said as she moved the steampunk machine to a side table.

"Extraordinary," the woman said as she lay down on her stomach across Jet's client table. There was the black outline of a tiger across her creamy white back. She was looking at the dials on the power supply of my mod. "Does it work?" she asked.

"Yeah, it does," I answered, holding out my hand.

Jet took my hand and peeled open the gauze. "You did this?" she asked as she led me by the hand to her after-station. She cleaned off the tattoo with alcohol and rubbed something else into it. The black ink popped against my glistening skin. She studied it appraisingly. "That's really good. It looks simple; but a perfect circle is really hard to do, especially if you've never tattooed before." She put fresh gauze on my hand. "Girl, you can apprentice under me anytime," she said with a smile.

"Hey, I thought that was my position," the woman with the half-drawn tiger on her back said.

Jet smacked her on the rear. "And you better remember

that, my love," she said before she pulled on her gloves.

Figures, Jet has a girlfriend. I don't know why I thought she could like me. I started backing toward the door.

"Did you use a stencil?" Jet asked.

"Stencil?" It hadn't even occurred to me to use any kind of stencil or even to draw it freehand first. I just did it. Of course, I'd seen Grandfather and Jet work before. They usually drew up the design and then copied it onto a stencil, which they applied to the client's skin. Then they inked over the lines.

"Don't tell me you did that freehand." Jet looked incredulous.

"Show me how to make a stencil," I said, a new hummingbird flitting around in my brain.

Stencil. Ink. Paper. That just might work.

13

Now Who's Being Paranoid?

Therapeutic Statement 42-03282028-11
Subject: JAMES, NORA EMILY, 15
Facility: HAMILTON DETENTION CENTER TFC-42

Winter sent a message that she had a surprise for Micah and me after school.

Her surprise was set up on the low table in the pagoda at the center of her garden.

"It's just the guts so far," Winter explained. "But it works. Later I'll fix it so you can feed the original into a slot and it'll all print out."

One part of the contraption looked like a scanner or copier. It was a wide, low box with a glass top and a slot below. The other part looked like a big tin can with a crank handle.

Winter pulled on some cheap disposable gloves and laid the comic facedown on the glass. She pressed a button, and a light scanned the image from below; nothing unusual, but instead of paper a shiny sheet of goo oozed out of the slot.

"Gelatin," Winter said. "It's a stencil." The stencil had an impression of the comic. Winter lifted the glass and showed us, Micah mostly, how she'd put an old dot matrix printer, a piece of junk from the 1990s, under the hood to cut the stencil. This kind of printer used real pressure rather than ink or light to make an image. A roll of home-made gelatin-backed paper was also under the hood.

Winter held up the stencil to the light. "If you wanted to," she told Micah, "you could freehand right on this with a stylus." Then she put the stencil faceup on the tin can thing, clipping it in place with the tiny metal holders that were screwed into the can. She cranked the handle slowly. The contraption printed out a fresh black-and-white copy of *Memento*.

"The ink's from Grandfather's shop. He makes it himself. I had to tweak it a little for print."

Micah snatched up the copy.

"It's kind of messy," I said, straining to look over his shoulder. Some of the lines weren't that crisp, but it still looked good.

"I probably need to put more drying agent in the ink," Winter said. "Plus, it'll get better the more we do it."

Micah held up the paper to the light. "I bet I can touch up the master with a razor blade." He squinted at the stencil on the drum. "You know, this would be great for T-shirts or posters."

"It still seems like way too much trouble," I said.

"People used this kind of printing for underground magazines and comics way before copiers and the Internet," Winter said. She went off about something called a mimeograph machine and the history of antiestablishment magazines.

"Did your grandpa tell you this, too?" I asked, a little tired of her knowing everything.

"No," she said, surprised. "Jet did. She runs Grandfather's tattoo shop down the block. And her girlfriend, the reporter. She knew about the magazines. The shop has an old thermofax machine that Jet let me look at. It makes stencils that you press on the skin and then tattoo over. Same idea."

"Now, that's glossy," Micah said with a low whistle. He started to examine his forearm for optimum tattoo placement.

"You didn't tell her what you were doing, did you?" I asked.

"Now who's being paranoid?" Winter laughed.

I turned red.

"Don't worry. I told her it was for an art history project."

I had to laugh at that.

*　　*　　*

We printed about two hundred copies of the first ever issue of *Memento*. And Winter was right. It did get better looking the more we printed.

"We should've used colored paper," I said. It was all I could think to add.

*   *   *

The next morning I stood in line at the security checkpoint at school with a stack of freshly inked paper tucked into my bag. Winter and Micah were doing the same. My heart raced as my bag passed through the scanner; but the cop assigned to the school, a big, sandy-haired guy, just stood there watching the rent-a-cops work the machine. They all seemed bored out of their minds.

Micah, Winter, and I visited the bathrooms—separately, of course—and stealthily placed a handful of *Memento*s on the toilet in each stall, careful to appear as if we were just using the facilities. The school has cameras everywhere—except in the stalls. Micah thought that wasn't so much to preserve our privacy as to keep the pervs and pedophiles on the security staff to a minimum. It wasn't an elegant solution to the distribution problem, but it was the best we could come up with.

14

This Is Me Not Nipping It in the Bud

Therapeutic Statement 42-03282028-11
Subject: JAMES, NORA EMILY, 15
Facility: HAMILTON DETENTION CENTER TFC-42

Homeroom was quiet—except for the drone of Homeland Teen News in the background. HTN is this 'cast that all Homeland-owned high schools have to run in the mornings. Today's lead story was about teamwork on and off the field. Nobody was watching. I tried to cram for a Spanish quiz but ended up just staring at the words while I listened for something. I don't know what. Maybe a swarm of security guards crashing through the hallways. A black helicopter landing on the roof. All I heard were the usual whispers of my classmates and the rustle of paper. I let out a breath and tried to focus on the vocabulary words. Micah and Winter were just being their paranoid selves, I told myself.

Mr. Finchly got up from his desk, which was unusual, and

started walking down the aisle toward me. He moved with deliberate speed, like a police car moves right before its lights start flashing. I imagined myself sitting in the office, police by the door, my father storming in. Then Mr. Finchly brushed past me. I heard him stop a few desks behind me.

"Mr. Jameson, is there something you'd like to share with the class?" Mr. Finchly's crisp British accent echoed in the now silent room.

Rick Jameson replied, "Why yes, sir, there is." He held up a familiar sheet of paper.

Mr. Finchly snatched up Rick's copy of *Memento* and read it quickly. In my head, I could hear the helicopters hitting the roof and cops swarming the halls, but I couldn't turn away. I had to see his reaction.

"Where did you get this?" Mr. Finchly asked.

I couldn't tell what he was thinking, but I thought I was going to hurl.

"They're all over the place," someone else—Catrina Jackson, I think—replied. Other kids agreed, saying they found it in the bathroom, hallway, café courtyard, locker rooms.

I forgot how to breathe for a minute.

The bell rang. Nobody moved.

Finally, Mr. Finchly turned on his heel, wadded up the paper, and tossed it in the trash can at the front of the room.

"Well," he said, turning back to the class. "What are you waiting for? Get out of here."

* * *

On my way to Spanish, I started to think it was all going to be all right. I even relaxed enough to get a B on the quiz.

After third period I met my girls outside the yearbook room. We started talking about Mercedes Rios breaking up with Trey Collins on *Behind the Gates*. I hadn't told anyone yet we were moving. I couldn't think that far ahead—even if it was only eighteen days. I hated the idea of leaving my girls, though I knew they'd be so behind the move. I'd be their ticket into compound life.

"Oh, she'd never marry him," I said when Maia brought up Trey's brother, Stone, as a possible replacement; but I didn't finish the thought. We could hear lockers slamming and unfamiliar voices down the hall toward the gym.

The school cop and his squad of rent-a-cops were searching lockers. Actually, the real cop watched as the others did all the work.

"I bet it's because of that *Memento* comic," Abby said.

"Oh yeah, everyone's got one."

"Someone ran off copies in the library."

"My cousin sent it to my mobile just before third period—and she goes to a private school across town."

Wow. I had no idea it would spread this fast. Or at all. It had become self-replicating, like the viruses we were studying in biology. I started getting that queasy feeling again.

"Hey, isn't that your skate-punk art history partner?" Maia asked, pointing to a security guard frisking a kid. Micah.

Micah, however, was grinning as they patted him down. I didn't dare move, even if I could. He opened his bag for them as if he didn't have a thing in the world to hide. They turned out books and papers and candy bars and even dirty socks, but no sketch pads. He winked at me as he stuffed all his belongings back into his messenger bag.

"Girl, he likes you," Abby said, giving me a little shove.

I blushed, and Maia told me I'd better nip that in the bud.

I didn't say anything. All I could see was that big, sandy-haired cop staring at me.

The rest of the school day dragged on forever.

• • •

That afternoon I waited in our usual spot in the library, but Micah didn't show. The school cop did. He sauntered in about five minutes after I sat down. He poked his head into the librarian's office. Ms. Curtis is kind of cute, so I thought maybe he was just hitting on her. She giggled, and I relaxed a bit. I opened one of the big art books from the perpetual stack on the table. No one seems to tidy up this place. The book was about kinetic sculpture. I turned the page, and a piece of paper fluttered out. *They're watching us.* I stuffed the note back into the book and looked up to see the cop smiling at me as he headed out of the library.

"I see Mr. Wallenberg stood you up." It was Ms. Curtis. She'd emerged from her office to watch the cop leave. "Oh, don't worry about him." I wasn't sure if she meant the officer or Micah. She looked at me differently then.

"You know, we have similar taste in men," she said.

I was so not having this conversation with the school librarian. I grabbed my bag and stood up.

"We fall for the ones our friends—and family—don't get," she added with a sad smile.

"I've got to go." I left the library.

But then I thought, *Maybe she has something there.* Micah was not who Dad or my friends would pick for me. Still. She was like thirty-five or something. It was not the same thing at all.

But Micah was right. Someone was watching us, although maybe not for the reasons he imagined.

15

A Man Can Dream

Therapeutic Statement 42-03282028-12
Subject: WALLENBERG, MICAH JONAS, 15
Facility: HAMILTON DETENTION CENTER TFC-42

Dreams suck. Not all dreams do, obviously. But this one did. Big-time. Most mornings I don't even remember them. I just roll out of bed and see what's for breakfast. Okay, I feed the cat, do my chores, shower, and then see what's cooking. By the time I'm shoveling oatmeal into my mouth, any trace of a dream is out of my head.

This time, though, it was like something important was there, something I couldn't quite see, as if a wall were blocking it. I remember being in a crowd of people, all way taller than me. They were moving and shouting, not angry shouts but more like chanting. A guy—I think it was my dad—lifted me up and put me on a fence or wall so I could see over the crowd. He told me to stay put as the crowd started to surge forward, carrying him with it. All I could see were heads. Hundreds of them. Then there were sirens. And angry shouting. And shots. Smoke. People running. A man called my name. And then nothing. This big, fat wall of nothingness I couldn't see around.

I sketched what I remembered, meaning to show Nora later. Somehow that thought made me feel pretty mellow. Glossy even.

Then Mrs. Brooks knocked on the door. I knew it was her because Mom was working the night shift. Again.

"Young man," Mrs. Brooks said in that mock stern voice she puts on to get me to do stuff. "You're going to be late for school if you don't shake a leg. And you promised me some firewood for the ovens. We're making a big batch today."

I could already smell the bread baking across the square.

"I'm up," I told her.

"Sure you are." She chuckled. "I saved you some muffins for breakfast. Those Peterson kids eat enough for an army."

Mrs. Brooks always has my back.

I rolled out of my cot, banging my cast on the dresser that doubles for my desk. Our shack is a definite improvement over living in our car, but I still miss a real, person-sized bed. I pulled on the cleanest-smelling T-shirt I could find out of the pile on the floor, fed Mr. Mao, and wrestled a shopping cart out to the woodpile.

Sometimes we used salvage wood, the stuff we'd ripped out of old houses that was too damaged to use again. Today we had proper logs for the bake ovens. A guy traded us a truckload for some bathroom fixtures and a half-dozen loaves of rosemary garlic sourdough. Mrs. Brooks has connections.

I wheeled the cart over to the pavilion and told Mrs. Brooks I'd get the rest after school.

"Sure you will," she said, nodding. She handed me a warm paper bag filled with blueberry muffins and a to-go cup of coffee. The smell of the blueberries and the coffee (and that little dash of vanilla the old lady dabbed on her wrists every morning) was the smell of pure love.

"Marry me, Mrs. Brooks," I said as I slung my bag over my shoulder.

"Get to school, child," she said, this time not so stern. She pointed toward the gate.

I stopped on the King footbridge just outside the school gates to eat all three muffins and gulp down the coffee. The late bell rang as I was licking the crumbs out of the paper bag.

Morning classes were a real snooze as usual. I like my afternoon classes—art and shop; but the morning ones— English and algebra, especially—give me a headache. I know I'm not stupid, but sometimes I have trouble wrapping my brain around stuff that I can't do with my hands. Or my mouth. I dozed off while Mr. Finchly droned on about the attack on Pearl Harbor in the 1940s.

At lunch I caught up with my usual crew. Spike. Richie. Little Steven. Velvet. Winter. And Little Steven's brother, Big Steven. I know; his parents are creatively challenged. Velvet's parents named her Anne Marie. No one knows

Spike's real name. We suspect it's something very long, Greek, and unpronounceable.

We usually sit at the back table against the wall. It's good for people watching and sketching. And the jocks don't bother us there. Well, the jocks don't pick on us too much since Little Steven grew a foot and half last summer and pierced his nose.

Anyway, Spike was ribbing me about the comic. "We know you drew it," he said. "Dude, it has you all over it."

Spike is into art, too. Clothes are his medium, he says. He likes spattering stuff on T-shirts and jeans and calling it street wear. Some of it is okay. Like today. He was wearing a *Memento* T-shirt—and, if I knew Spike, he was planning to make many more. Total badass.

"Don't worry," Velvet said, leaning over the table toward me. She was sporting one of Spike's nonpolitical painted tees over a really short skirt and black tights. "We'd never give you up."

Winter glared at her, and she backed off.

"But we're curious," she said, looking at Winter, "about this new chick you've been hanging out with."

Winter was suddenly very interested in her burrito, but I caught her cutting me a sidelong glance as Velvet pressed for details. I couldn't tell what Winter was thinking; but then again, I generally suck at mind reading.

"Oh, leave him alone," Richie chimed in. "The man can dream." He was watching someone as he said this. I glanced up. It was Nora. She was making her way to the salad bar. She looked very little-girl-lost today.

Richie started talking about a gig his band had next weekend. He plays bass in a retro band that mostly plays Bar Mitzvahs. No one in the band is old enough to be out past curfew let alone get into a bar. So they play the Mitzvah-Sweet Sixteen-Quinceañera circuit. This new gig was in the Cherry Falls compound, but Richie's dad didn't want to spring for the chip just so he could play there. Richie nudged me and said something about a new song he wanted to lay on the compound crowd. I nodded like I was listening, but I was watching Nora.

She was looking shaky as she sat down with her friends. One of them—Maia, the tennis player—glared at me. They're all look-good-on-the-college-app types. Everything they do is prep for some golden future laid out before them. I watched Nora pick at her salad. She looked like she was going to puke or bolt any second.

Man, I wished I'd never messed with Nora's head back at TFC. She was too good for that. Too good for me.

It Takes a Junkyard

Therapeutic Statement 42-03282028-11
Subject: JAMES, NORA EMILY, 15
Facility: HAMILTON DETENTION CENTER TFC-42

The bones rattled like a sack of chicken legs in a Brooks Brothers suit. The air smelled like burning books. Car alarms wailed all along Market Street. Mom wasn't there to cover my eyes. Micah was there instead, and he made me look. At the socks. At the silver watch stopped at ten past two. At the book with *Memento* written on its spine. I knelt and touched its cover. It burst into a cloud of ash, covering me in fine gray silt, choking me until I woke up gasping for air.

I skipped breakfast.

That day was so dreary. I was waiting for something to happen, waiting for school to end, waiting to see Micah. Just waiting.

In homeroom, HTN ran a story on the extracurricular

activities that could get you into your dream college. Then a Homeland guy reminded us that all student publications must be approved by the board. Some of the kids in class booed. The only student pub we have now is the yearbook.

* * *

I caught a glimpse of Micah during lunch as I was getting my salad. He was sitting at the far table with his artsy, weird friends, which included Winter. Her spikes were red now. She didn't look at me, but Micah did.

"I told you to nip that in the bud," Maia said as we sat down at our usual table. I knew she meant Micah.

"There's nothing to nip," I said as coolly as I could.

"Uh-huh." She didn't sound convinced.

"Did you hear Zack Smith got suspended for making copies of that comic?" Abby asked. "The cops even thought he wrote it."

That made Maia laugh. "He couldn't even spell *memento*."

"He'll be okay," Hunter said. "His mom's a big wheel at TFC."

The conversation continued like that for a while. I didn't say anything. The girls talked about several kids either getting detention (little *d*, the school variety) or suspended for trying to send *Memento* to friends. Maia kept looking at me. It wasn't like me to be so quiet, I know, but I just didn't feel up to the chatter. Then one of the guys from the next table said he'd heard Mike Delaney wasn't here today because his folks had lost it when they'd found his copy of *Memento*. They were talking about putting him in private school.

It was getting hot and close and way too noisy in the cafeteria. I told the girls I wasn't feeling well and practically sprinted to the trash can to toss out my lunch. Scraping the lettuce and creamy French dressing into the smelly waste bin didn't help. The room started to spin.

"Are you okay?" a voice behind me asked. It was Micah. He slid his bloodred spaghetti into the trash.

I had to get air. I made for the door out to the courtyard. The band geeks eat lunch out there. I headed for the big apple tree by the edge of the school grounds. The breeze felt amazing against my hot skin. I leaned up against the knobbly bark of the tree and watched the squirrels scamper and the blossoms begin to fall to the ground.

Then I felt something cold being pressed into my hands. Micah was handing me a chilled bottle of water. I drank the whole thing in one big, greedy gulp.

"It comes back up on you sometimes," he said as quietly as the breeze rustling through the trees. "The things we're supposed to forget."

I nodded. We sank down into the grass by the tree. I didn't bother to see if anyone was watching us. It felt good just sitting there in the grass. With him.

"It pisses me off." I said it a little louder than I'd intended. "I don't feel safe anywhere anymore. Not home. Not school," I added at a slightly more reasonable volume. I thought about mentioning the move to Los Palamos but didn't.

Micah nodded. I told him about the dream I kept having. He nodded again.

We sat there watching the squirrels chase each other along the security fence that separated us from the outside world.

"Want to see where I feel safe?" Micah asked after a long silence. "You've got to swear to keep it secret."

I nodded. I couldn't imagine where he'd take me, but I felt safe with him.

He said it wasn't far—and we needed a few hours off. We could be back in time for the car service to pick me up, same as usual.

Believe it or not, I'd never ditched before; but getting out of school isn't a problem, Micah explained as we went through the security checkpoint.

"The corporation that runs this place just cares about liability on campus. They don't want you to bring in anything disruptive or explosive—or steal anything expensive." He stopped talking and smiled oh so innocently as the rent-a-cop scanned our bags.

From the school we walked a couple of blocks, across an old pedestrian bridge that ran over the highway, and then another block to a place called Black Dog Architectural Reclamation and Bakery. The bakery part hung below the main sign on a painted wooden panel.

"Your safe place is a junkyard," I said, astonished.

It was an old brick building with antique bathtubs and stone gargoyles in one window—and loaves of bread in another. Instead of going in the front door, Micah led me around the side to a wrought iron gate with an Authorized Personnel Only sign hanging on it. A stone wall seemed to encircle the actual junkyard part behind the building.

"Don't worry, I'm authorized," Micah said, laughing, as he pushed open the creaky gate.

Once inside, we wound our way through a maze of junk. Stacks of wrought iron fencing. More old-fashioned bath-tubs. Stained glass windows. Doors. As we turned a corner and I caught a whiff of fresh-baked bread, we ran into a black dog. A big one.

"Bridget, this is Nora," Micah told the dog. She sniffed me once and then ran back the way she had come, tail wagging as she trotted. "She won't allow strangers past this point without an introduction."

We emerged from the junk maze; and Micah opened another gate, this one with a dog flap at the bottom. Bells tinkled as he shut it behind us. Inside was something almost as surprising and wonderful as Winter's garden.

We stepped onto a neat green lawn with a stone path cutting through it to a brick square. There was a row of min-iature town houses on one side of the square and a covered pavilion on the other. The town houses looked like giant doll- or playhouse versions of the ones in my neighborhood. These were skinnier and much shorter—only one story, if that—but they had windows and shutters and even flower boxes. The exteriors were painted in alternating colors: blue, white, yellow, green. My first thought was that Mom would love these.

"Welcome to Black Dog Village," Micah said proudly, as if he'd created the place himself.

The smell of baking bread filled the air. Several people

waved to us. A group of small children played on the green lawn near the jungle gym while an older woman watched from her porch.

"Young man." A tall, wiry black woman with short gray hair steamed up to us. "What is your mother going to think, you coming home in the middle of the school day? And don't think she's not going to find out. And bringing a girl? A real pretty one at that."

I blushed.

"She's going to think I was hungry for some of that good rosemary sourdough bread you're baking, Mrs. Brooks, and maybe some of that stew." Micah turned on the charm, charm I didn't know he had.

Micah introduced me to Mrs. Brooks. She laughed and said she was still going to tell his mother. Micah didn't seem very worried about that.

"Amelia," a skinny white girl in a sundress called from the pavilion, "I think the bread is done."

Mrs. Brooks shooed us toward the girl, who upon closer inspection must have been about thirty. She was opening the black iron door on a low brick oven. The heat and the warm-bready smell washed over me, and I realized I was starving.

"Those look good, honey," Mrs. Brooks told the woman. "Melinda is learning the trade," Mrs. Brooks explained to me, "in exchange for showing me how to do pottery so I can make flowerpots and plates and such." She pointed to a stack of pretty light blue and creamy brown bowls stacked by the oven.

"Oh, I want to learn, too," Micah said.

"You want to learn everything, child," Mrs. Brooks replied. "Did he tell you he learned how to weld so he could make the iron flower boxes and the jungle gym?" she asked me.

I watched Micah as he ran his finger over the swirly texture of one of the bowls. I noticed he latches on to some things, things that intrigue him, I guess, with this sweet, open eagerness.

"Most times he needs a kick in the pants to finish one thing before he's off to the next," Mrs. Brooks said, chuckling.

Micah ignored her as he examined a big blue plate with this greenish glaze on it. It was glossy in all senses of the word.

"Now that Winter girl," Mrs. Brooks added. "She's good at getting things done." She pointed to the solar panels on the roof of the pavilion. Mrs. Brooks looked at me as if trying to judge what I had to offer. "In the words of Maya Angelou, 'Nothing works unless you do,'" she said finally. I wasn't sure if that was directed at Micah or me.

While she'd been talking, the other woman, Melinda, had pulled out a half-dozen round loaves of golden brown bread with a big wooden paddle. She laid them out to cool with another half-dozen or so loaves. She took one of the hot loaves and cut off a couple hunks for us and wrapped them in a clean towel.

"There's still some stew left," Melinda said as she handed us the bread. Her voice was as airy as wind chimes.

Micah scooped up the stew and motioned me toward the tables. Most of them seemed to be made out of doors. A couple of people said hi to us. One ladled out something from a big pot into two bowls, and Micah and I sat down at a pale yellow table with GENTS stenciled on it.

The stew in the bowl looked and smelled really good, but not as good as the bread. I wolfed it down while Micah told me about the Village. His talking didn't slow his eating at all. He sopped up stew with a hunk of bread and inhaled it without missing a breath.

The Village is only a couple years old, Micah explained. Mr. Shaw, the owner of the salvage yard (and Bridget), let them stay there as long as there was no trouble and they helped out in the business when needed. Micah had helped collect salvage from house renovations many times. Most people throw out the beautiful old wood and iron and even stained glass when they put in fancy new kitchens and bathrooms or security measures like blast windows and fortified media rooms. Some folks still care about preserving old houses, and they buy fixtures and fencing from Black Dog—but not as much as they used to, which is why Mr. Shaw was cool with having people live on the property in exchange for a little work. Then business had gotten so bad that he and his family had lost their house and moved into the Village themselves.

All residents have to have some skill and be approved by everyone before they move in. Micah and his mom had moved in last year, he explained, after they'd lost their apartment downtown and lived on the streets for a few months. For some reason his mom's security score is very low, as are a lot of folks' scores in the Village. That means they have to buy a lot of things the old-fashioned way: with cash. Without a good security score, you can't buy or rent a decent place. Or even get some jobs. And forget about getting an ID chip.

Anyway, after living out of shelters or in their car, Micah and his mom ended up here on the recommendation of Mrs. Brooks. Micah's mom and Mrs. Brooks had worked at the same retirement home a while back. Mrs. Brooks had been the chef there before some big company took over.

"I think Mrs. Brooks used to teach English before she lost her house," Micah said as he licked the bowl. "She's always quoting poetry at me."

Micah's mom is still a nurse at Sunny Oaks. And when she gets home, she takes care of everyone in the Village, at least until they have to go to the emergency room. She's stitched up cuts, taped up sprains, nursed people through the flu, and even delivered a baby or two.

After we finished our stew, Micah showed me the gardens and playgrounds. The Village grows fresh vegetables and herbs, and barters or pools its money for meat and flour and sugar. Most of the residents have jobs—or they work for Mr. Shaw. They just need a safe place to live.

We sat on the top of the jungle gym Micah'd made out of scrap metal and wrought iron, and I could understand why he felt safe there. I felt safe there, too. Maybe it was just the bread warming my insides. Or the smell of lavender from the gardens. Or the murmur of friendly voices. Or the sight of children playing. I reached out and took his hand.

He looked pleasantly surprised.

"What about your dad?" I asked.

He hesitated and then said, "I don't really remember my dad." I could feel him wanting to wriggle free from my hand. "I know I should. I was like five or six when he left. Mom won't talk about it, but she swears she didn't pill me into forgetting."

"Do you believe her?" I asked him. I asked myself, *Could she have secretly pilled him? She's a nurse. They might have the TFC pill where she works. She could have slipped it into his oatmeal. Maybe.* But then I thought, *no. If she could do that, she wouldn't have bothered to take him to TFC at all. Besides, like the TFC doctor explained, the pill alone wasn't enough to make you forget. You had to talk about the specific memory.*

Micah shrugged. "But even if she didn't, I don't want to forget anything else."

Micah slid down the jungle gym to the ground. He gave me his good hand to guide me. The cast on his bum arm was beginning to look pretty tattered. He'd covered up the *Memento* with a big snake, just like Mr. Yamada had on his arm.

"We should do the next issue on your story," I said as I slid to the ground in front of him, my hand still in his. My momentum carried me right into him, face-to-face. My breath caught as I inhaled him; and before I realized what I was doing (or maybe I did), I leaned in ever so slightly and brushed his lips with mine. He tasted of bread and rosemary. We lingered there a moment—until we heard someone clear her throat.

"Young man—and young lady—you'd better get your butts back to school." We turned to see Mrs. Brooks, her arms folded. She stood there until we started moving. But as we headed toward the gate, I swore I heard a low, warm chuckle behind us.

*　　*　　*

"What were you saying?" Micah asked as we wound our way back through the maze of junk to the outer gate.

I had to think for a second. "Your story," I said. "We should do it next."

"We can't mention the Village," he said, a little panicky. "We're technically not squatting, but we can't get Mr. Shaw in trouble with the city. He's not really supposed to have so many people here."

"No, I was thinking more about the not-remembering-your-father part," I said. "It makes your story make sense—just like my mom's memory made mine make sense."

"You're pretty smart for a prep," he teased, his hand resting on my hip.

We were crossing the pedestrian bridge again. I stopped to read the plaque. The bridge was dedicated to Dr. Martin Luther King Jr. as a symbolic (and actual) bridge between neighborhoods. Micah put his arm loosely around me as I read. I think he was about to kiss my cheek when the school bell rang. I pulled away. I'm not sure why. It was like the real world was calling.

"Library. Usual time," I said over my shoulder as I walked back toward school. I left him standing there.

I tried not to think about his arm around me. Or his lips against mine. Instead I thought about his story. I could see it in my head how I wanted to do it. I started writing it out in English class when I should've been taking notes on the history of the Globe Theater. We'd start where we left off, with Micah getting hit by the black van, spitting out the pill at TFC, and then telling me—or my character—later about his father. And vowing never to forget anything ever again.

*   *   *

He was late. I was sitting in his usual place—back to the art stacks, a pile of books in front of me—as I scribbled away. He didn't say much as he slid into my usual seat. I didn't look up. I just kept writing. Micah shifted in his seat, and I could feel his uneasiness next to me. He reached for his bag and started to leave.

"Where do you think you're going?" I asked as I pushed the pad of paper in front of him.

A big smile spread across his lips, and he plunked himself back into the seat. I'd used stick figures to rough out the action. The art was crap, but it was his story. He started sketching immediately.

I noticed Ms. Curtis was watching us more closely than usual. I casually knocked a book off the ever-present stack of coffee-table-sized tomes on our table. Micah took the hint and covered up his sketch pad.

"How are we going to get the comic into the school this

time?" I asked as I put a book about medieval churches back on top of the stack. "We'll all get searched on the way in." In addition to the usual scans, security had been ransacking kids' bags this morning.

The students weren't happy about the new searches. I'd heard kids complaining about it in all my classes.

Maia had told me that one kid made himself a *Memento* T-shirt. But the guards had been so busy with the bags that they hadn't noticed what the guy was wearing.

Micah stared at the books in front of us. Then he picked up three of them and took them to the front desk. He checked them out from Ms. Curtis and came back to the table.

"She may not like what I'm going to do to them," Micah whispered to me as he stuffed the books into his bag.

*   *   *

The next day after school we took a new issue of *Memento* and three hollowed-out art books to Winter's garden.

Micah would say he lost them and pay for the books at the end of the school year. He'd cut an eight-and-a-half-by-eleven-inch cavity in the center of each book, leaving enough whole pages at the front and back to pass a casual flip-through. He'd carefully preserved the insides and said he might rebind them or use them in some sort of collage. He'd been meaning to try some mixed-media pieces, anyway, he said.

There was one book for each of us.

He handed Winter a book on kinetic sculptures. "Can

I have the insides of this one?" she asked, rifling through the book.

I got the one on medieval churches of Europe. Micah's was on graphic novels of the twentieth century.

Eager to get started, Micah scanned the original comic and then carefully inspected the stencil.

"Let him do that," Winter said to me, putting down her book. "I want to show you the solar sails."

This was a new one, her wanting to show *me* something. Did that mean she'd decided I was okay? I stopped for a split second. Or did she want to tell me to stay away from Micah? I followed her out to the garden.

The fourth sculpture had progressed from a pile of canvases and circuits to an odd rigging of colorful rectangular sails or curtains. Each color and shape, she said, would play a different note or tone when the sun hit it. Like a solar wind chime.

"It doesn't seem as disturbing as the other ones," I remarked. "It's cool, but . . ."

Then she turned it on. The sounds were these glossy ring tones, slowed down or tweaked out to sound like whispers, haunting whispers of the outside world, those tinkles of annoyingly cheerful sound that remind you that someone can always call you, can always watch you somehow, can always find you.

"It's perfect," I said, looking at her. I noticed the dark circles under her eyes, one of which was twitching slightly, as if it were holding back some surge of energy. It took a brilliant, spidery mind to think of this, of everything in this garden.

The music, if you could call it that, began to take on a darker tone as a cloud passed over the sun.

"I'm sorry I brought up your mom the other day," Winter said, staring at her creation.

"That's okay," I replied almost automatically. I hadn't expected an apology. "She doesn't remember your parents," I added quietly.

"But—," Winter started to say. Then she got it. "Oh."

There wasn't much else to say, and that *oh* hung like a note between us for a long moment.

"We should do your story for the next issue," I said to break the silence.

She shook her head but kept staring at her solar sails. I didn't press her. I figured she didn't want to get her parents in any deeper trouble than they already were.

The music got even creepier in the silence between us.

"Enough of that." Winter shuddered as she clicked off the sound. But she was smiling.

We stepped back into the gazebo just as Micah was printing off the first test page. Winter and I read it over his shoulder as he held it up. Again, I got that feeling. Like we had something good here. Winter was quiet, her smile gone.

"I didn't know that about your dad," she whispered. Then she muttered something about putting more drying agent in the ink and headed into the house.

*   *   *

That night I dreamed about kissing Micah at the prom. His tux was from Goodwill, and it smelled vaguely of old books and rosemary.

The All-Devouring "It"

Therapeutic Statement *42-03282028-13*
Subject: *NOMURA, WINTER, 14*
Facility: *HAMILTON DETENTION CENTER TFC-42*

Step. Whir. Step. Whir.

I saw the figure in black run along the rooftops. Then he grabbed on to this curtain that was hanging there between two buildings; and he started Tarzaning across, handful by handful. Just as he was halfway, he looked down at me. It was Sasuke-san. He smiled. Then I heard a horrendous sound. The fabric ripped under his weight. He grabbed another swath of curtain, but it tore free as he swung himself in the direction of the other building. Grandfather tumbled toward me.

I woke up in a panic. I ran through the house looking for Grandfather, the *step-whir* in my head growing louder with each empty room. The sound blurred into the frenzy of hummingbird wings fighting against a strong wind. I found him in my gazebo, a pot of tea in front of him, his head resting on his hand, his eyes closed. He was dressed in black.

"Ojiisan," I whispered.

"You haven't called me that since you were a little girl," he said, his eyes fluttering open.

Ojiisan is about the limit of my Japanese. It means "grandfather." He'd offered to teach me, but I'd always resisted learning more. I thought if I knew the language, my *ojiisan* might send me far, far away from him, all the way to Japan, where he thought I'd be safer.

"What's wrong, Win-chan?" he asked. He poured a cup of tea, chamomile by the smell, and pushed it toward me. "Talk to me."

Feeling very much like a little girl—and not really minding it—I sat down at the low table in front of my grandfather.

"I dreamed I lost you," I said in a small voice as I stared into the depths of the teacup. He put his hand over mine. "On the stupid Curtain Cling," I added, feeling much more my cranky teenage self.

He laughed. The *step-whir* in my head disappeared, and I noticed his hands weren't rough like they usually were. He was wearing his gloves, the half-fingered leather, grippy ones. He only wore them for one thing.

"I hope you weren't patrolling by yourself tonight," I said, squeezing his hand. I knew Grandfather had been doing the neighborhood watch thing after curfew for a while now. He didn't like to talk about it.

Grandfather nodded wearily. "You know, you look like

your mother," he said as he peeled off the skintight gloves, changing the subject like always.

"Talk to me, Ojiisan," I said, pouring him another cup of tea.

"I'm just tired, Win-chan." He took a long sip of tea. "Tired of watching and waiting. Tired of feeling like there's nothing I can do."

I knew he wasn't talking about patrolling the neighborhood. He was talking about the "it" we never talked about. The big, all-devouring it. The fact that Spring and Brian Nomura are never coming home. No matter what we do. No matter how much money and how many lawyers we throw at the system. It had ground them up. Not even the mighty Nomura Corporation, the biggest mobile company in North America, could buy Mom and Dad out of whatever trouble they were in.

*   *   *

The *step-whir* was back. I kissed my grandfather on the forehead and told him to go to bed. I had to go do something. Anything. Tinker in my shop. Work on a sculpture. Print more comics. Just like my *ojiisan*. He worked, patrolled, and ran that damn Sasuke course to escape the all-devouring it of our lives.

Looking back at him, still half dozing at the table, I knew it wasn't enough for either of us. But what else could we do?

"By the way," he said, yawning. "My support group

wants to talk to you." He said it as if the thought both amused and exhausted him.

Damn. I thought he'd quit that stupid group. Not long after Mom and Dad disappeared, Grandfather joined this support group for the families of the missing. I thought it was a colossal waste of time. It couldn't bring my parents back, and there was no way I was going to some touchy-feely, wallow-in-each-other's-pain group therapy thing. He looked so tired, though, I didn't have the heart to argue about it then.

"It's not what you think," he added.

"We'll talk in the morning," I said. My plan, however, was to be out of the house long before he got up. I had shit to do, anyway.

Later, I stuffed the latest issue of *Memento* into a hollowed-out copy of *Kinetic Sculptures of Twentieth-Century Europe*.

Not that this will do any good, I thought. *Nothing ever changes for the better.*

The comic's pages smelled like a new tattoo.

18

I Wasn't Worried

Therapeutic Statement 42-03282028-11
Subject: JAMES, NORA EMILY, 15
Facility: HAMILTON DETENTION CENTER TFC-42

The next morning, with a couple hundred freshly inked copies of *Memento* hidden in hollowed-out library books, we approached the bag search at the security checkpoint into school. The sandy-haired cop—Officer Bell, his tag said—searched my bag personally.

"*Medieval Churches*?" he asked, an eyebrow arched.

"Art history project," I said calmly. I waited for him to open it, ready to run if he did. He didn't.

He put it back in my bag and moved on to the next kid.

I left a stack of papers tucked behind a toilet in the second-floor ladies' room. And when I bumped into my girls before homeroom, I whispered that I'd heard *Memento* was back in school. "A brand-new issue. Check the bathrooms." I assume Micah and Winter did something similar.

By Spanish class the school was awash in paper. Our paper. And it was all anybody could talk about. But they didn't stop with *Memento*.

"You know, we ought to do something, too," the kid behind me said to his friend when our teacher left the room. We were supposed to be watching a 'cast about Costa Rica. In Spanish.

"But what?"

"We could boycott TFC," the girl next to me said.

"Or we could petition to bring back the school paper," another girl said.

"Or we could plan an epic Senior Prank," a senior interjected from the back of the room. His friends "oh-yeah"ed in response. One of the guys had on an ugly yellow Homeland Inc. shirt. He and about a dozen other students had worn *Memento* T-shirts this morning, but the principal confiscated them and made the kids wear Homeland ones instead.

I concentrated really hard on the screen.

*   *   *

Still, no black helicopters or SWAT teams swept down over the school that day. I did see the rent-a-cops searching lockers—and Micah—again, but I wasn't worried this time.

At least not until I found Officer Bell waiting for Micah and me in the library after school.

19

Hi, My Name Is Nora J.

Therapeutic Statement 42-03282028-11
Subject: JAMES, NORA EMILY, 15
Facility: HAMILTON DETENTION CENTER TFC-42

At first I didn't realize it was him. He was sitting in Micah's usual spot with one of the big coffee-table art books propped up in front of him. One about surrealists, I think. I sat down beside him just as Micah breezed into the library on his skateboard. That's when the book came down, and the door closed behind Micah.

"I'd like you two to come with me," Officer Bell said firmly. He looked more annoyed than anything. "And don't think about skating out of here. I know where you live. Both of you," he said, looking meaningfully at Micah.

So, I thought, it had finally come. My father would storm into the police station. We'd be expelled or grounded or both. I resigned myself to my fate. And Micah's. He held my hand as we walked out of the library. I let him. It didn't matter now what anyone thought about Micah and me.

Officer Bell locked up the library—Ms. Curtis was nowhere in sight—and let us stash our stuff in our lockers. "Leave your mobile," he added before I closed the door. He directed us out the staff entrance to the parking garage where his car sat idling. No one saw us.

He drove for about ten minutes with the back windows of his patrol car blacked out. Then he let us out in an alley behind a brick building.

"Is this a police station?" I whispered to Micah.

He shook his head. And I knew what he was thinking, what I was now thinking. Detention. The big *D* variety. It wouldn't have a neon sign or valet parking. It could be anywhere, look like anything.

We both glanced up and down the alley. No cars. No people. We didn't have mobiles or any money. And I certainly didn't know where we were or where else to go but home or school—and as Officer Bell had so kindly pointed out, he knew where we lived.

He guided us toward some stairs leading to a basement. Micah squeezed my hand before we started down the steps. A bare bulb hung over a rusty metal door. And on that door was taped a piece of paper that said:

Memory Loss Support Group. 4 p.m.

Micah pulled open the door, and I could smell coffee. Burned coffee. And I could hear the sound of metal clacking against concrete or linoleum.

The cop gently pushed us into the room. It was long and narrow, with a little kitchen at one end. Fluorescent light bounced off freshly waxed floors. The walls were covered with kids' drawings, everything from colorful construction paper Noah's arks to macaroni crosses.

We were in a church basement.

"Help yourself," Officer Bell said, finally cracking a smile. "We'll be starting soon." He walked over to where people were setting out doughnuts and coffee on the breakfast bar in the kitchen.

Micah and I still didn't move. A handful of middle-aged men and women milled around, talking and sipping coffee. Some nodded in our general direction. One of them was the school librarian, Ms. Curtis. Micah nudged me and pointed toward the man setting out folding chairs. Vintage black hat. Tattoos snaking down his arms. It was Winter's grandfather.

"Mr. Yamada?" Micah moved to help him with the chairs, and I followed.

"What's going on?" I wanted some answers first.

"The group wanted to talk to you." Mr. Yamada acknowledged the cop with the slightest of nods. "Some thought it might be best to scare you a little first."

"Is Winter here, too?" Micah asked.

"Yes, I pulled her out of seventh period," Mr. Yamada said as he set a chair on the floor with a smack.

Micah seemed relieved, but my fear was quickly turning into anger.

"A memory loss group?" I pressed.

Mr. Yamada set the next chair down more gently. "It started out as a support group for those of us who lost someone to Detention," he explained. "Then others joined, mostly to vent about the way things are. And then it kind of grew into something else."

A man moved to the front of the room.

"Winter's over there," Mr. Yamada said, pointing toward the kitchen. "Showing them how to make proper coffee." He laughed.

His tone relaxed me somewhat, but I still wanted answers.

"Grab her and then come sit with me," he said. "The group will explain the rest.

"Don't worry," he added. "They're harmless. Relatively. But they're a bit full of themselves." He winked.

We did find Winter brewing her god-awful coffee. She started to say something, but Ms. Curtis told us to grab a doughnut and go sit down; Winter, too. Micah seized two chocolate crullers, and Winter grabbed a Styrofoam cup of her bitter brew and six sugar packets. Micah inhaled one of the crullers before offering me the other. I shook my head. I couldn't stomach anything. I watched him stuff the second cruller in his mouth and head back for more.

"I see you and Micah have worked things out," Ms. Curtis said. I had the feeling she'd seen me watching Micah. "You make an interesting couple."

"Oh, we're not—" I stopped because I knew I was busted. *Interesting?*

"I won't tell anyone," she whispered as Micah and Winter worked their way back toward us. Ms. Curtis herded everyone into the front row of seats.

Winter sat next to her grandfather, then Micah, then me. The librarian sat in one of the chairs by the podium at the front of the room. An older man stood at the podium and banged a gavel. Officer Bell slipped into the seat next to mine. He offered me a soda. I just shook my head.

"I call this meeting of the Memory Loss Support Group to order. Madam Secretary will review the minutes of the last meeting."

Ms. Curtis stood up and began to recite, "The MLSG met on February fifteenth at the Southside Methodist Church. The meeting lasted approximately fifty-three minutes. The Right Honorable Chairman Wilson Carver presided. We covered the following agenda items."

The librarian then rattled off a list of actions. The Black Van Committee reported three sightings last month, each in the vicinity of a later incident. (Micah caught my eye at the mention of the vans.) The Phone Tree Committee practiced a "fire drill" scenario. The Refreshment Committee decided to purchase doughnuts rather than bagels. Then she went through a litany of such-and-such moved this and such-and-such seconded it, this was tabled, and that was so noted.

"Is this a student council meeting?" Micah whispered to me.

"More like my parents' home owners' association," I whispered back. We'd had them at our house many, many times. Very dreary. I didn't know how they ever got anything done.

The cop stifled a laugh. Mr. Carver glared at us.

I looked at the old metal clock on the wall. Ms. Curtis had been going for ten minutes. And she was doing it all without looking at a piece of paper or a mobile. Pure memory.

"We don't commit anything to paper," the cop leaned in and whispered as if reading my thoughts. "Not that there's anything significant to put down."

The chairman glared at us again. Ms. Curtis sat down after another minute of yeahs and nays.

"We have a number of new items to cover today," Mr. Carver said without getting up. "We need more money for the Jonas Defense Fund in order to help the Trujillo family. Luis has been 'away' for nearly a year now, and Mercy was let go—again—last week. And we—"

Ms. Curtis leaned over and whispered something to the chairman. He sighed and nodded.

"Yes. Maybe we should dispense with our old business for the moment," he said, looking at us. "Our guests are getting restless. And I believe we need to get them back before their bedtimes."

Now I was really angry.

"Moving on to new business," the chairman said, looking at me. "We want you kids to stop producing your comic."

"What?" Micah almost spat out his fourth cruller.

"Sasuke-san?" Winter turned to her grandfather. Clearly she was as clueless as we were.

I stood up. "Excuse me, who are you guys anyway? And why the hell should we do what you say?" I kind of surprised myself.

Winter nodded at me as if she was actually impressed.

The chairman glared at Officer Bell again. "Didn't you tell them?"

"No." The cop shrugged. "This was your idea. You tell them."

Mr. Carver groaned. I kept standing.

"We're the underground," he said.

Winter snorted at that.

Mr. Carver visibly bristled. Then he focused on me and spoke calmly but firmly. "Young lady," he said.

I decided to sit down.

"We are an underground group of concerned citizens. . . ." He paused, looking for the words. "Let's just say we're more than a support group."

Ms. Curtis stood again. "In the beginning, all of us"—she looked at Mr. Yamada and a few others—"lost somebody to Detention. We all had a loved one or friend who was 'away,' as George so delicately put it. So we got together to support one another mentally, emotionally, and even financially. We still do that."

The chairman lowered his eyes.

"So?" I asked.

"The financial thing is the tricky part," Officer Bell said to me.

Mr. Yamada nodded. "It's illegal to give money to suspected terrorists."

"Koji and Doug are correct," Ms. Curtis said. "Which is why the Jonas Defense Fund—our legal defense fund—is so important and quite enough to get us all sent 'away,' too."

A strange look came over Micah.

"There's so much else we do—or could do," the chairman said. He looked like he wanted to say more but thought better of it. Plus, Ms. Curtis was glowering at him. "But let's not get into it right now." He turned to my friends and me. "The bottom line is that your activities, no matter how admirable, put ours at risk. That comic of yours has spread way outside Hamilton and DC, even beyond the East Coast."

I still didn't get how we put them at risk, but that was all they would say. They refused to tell us what else they did. They just made us promise to stop what we were doing. Micah was oddly quiet during the whole thing.

"And if we don't?" I asked.

"Officer Bell will have to do his job," the librarian said curtly.

Officer Bell shook his head slowly. "Katie, don't use me to threaten them."

Ms. Curtis did not look happy with him.

"I've had enough of this crap." Mr. Yamada stood up. "I only agreed to bring Winter to listen. You kids don't need to promise anything. We're leaving."

"Koji," the cop said, rising. "Let me take these two back to school." He and Winter's grandfather exchanged a look, and Mr. Yamada nodded.

"It's okay," he reassured us. "I trust Bell."

Winter just stood there next to her grandfather, staring at the cop with her X-ray vision as if trying to gauge his intentions. She didn't say a thing.

Micah and I ended up back in the cop car again. I wondered why Mr. Yamada—whose daughter and son-in-law had disappeared into Detention—would trust this cop. Why would any of them? And why would he be part of this so-called underground?

So I asked Officer Bell.

And to my surprise he told us.

"It was the black vans," he said without taking his eyes off the road.

Micah sat up when Bell said that.

Last year, Officer Bell said, back when he had still been on patrol, he'd noticed that whenever there was a bombing in his area, some witness always reported seeing a black van. None of the detectives had seemed to take this seriously. There are dozens of black vans at any one time in the city, they'd say. Then he'd seen one leaving the area near a bombing right after it happened. So he followed the van back to a building downtown and saw it go into an unmarked parking garage next to Tiffany's. He'd called it in, thinking the store might be the terrorists' next target. Nothing happened, though, and the next day he'd been bumped down to searching bags at our school.

"I started to watch for the vans on my off time," he said as we turned into the circular drive in front of the school. "I noticed Koji—Mr. Yamada—doing the same thing one evening. Eventually we talked, and he introduced me to the group. And Katie—Ms. Curtis." He blushed when he said her name.

"Thanks for telling us this," I said.

"I don't underestimate you like they do," he answered. "You kids may get more accomplished than that lot in there. Mind you, if it comes down to it, I may have to arrest you myself," he added.

"I still don't see why," I protested. "Free speech isn't against the law."

"Well, that doesn't seem to matter anymore," he said as he parked in the drop-off zone.

"What do the vans do?" Micah asked as I was reaching for the door handle. He'd been oddly quiet on the ride back and at the meeting, like he was someplace else. It was a good question.

Officer Bell didn't say anything for so long that I thought he wasn't going to answer. He just stared at the steering wheel.

"I'll show you," he finally said. "You wouldn't believe it otherwise. But I can't guarantee that we'll see anything the first time out." He told us to meet him next Tuesday at Winter's house. After dark. "I know you can get out after curfew," he added, looking at Micah.

Officer Bell let us back into school long enough to get our stuff and then he left us sitting on the front steps.

"He told us that story for a reason," I said to Micah as we waited for my car service. I'd had to call because we'd been a little late getting back to school. "Officer Bell must want us to use the black vans in *Memento*," I insisted.

"It would make a great story," Micah agreed. "But it won't make sense until we know exactly what the vans are up to."

"And who's behind them."

Micah nodded.

"Do you think they're Coalition terrorists?" I asked.

"Why would the cops cover for them?"

"Maybe they *are* cops. Some special bomb disposal unit."

"Then why wouldn't Bell have known that?"

I shrugged. "We should ask Winter. Maybe her grandfather told her something Bell left out."

Micah nodded again, but I could see his mind was racing ahead, kicking around the possibilities. He looked very cute lost in his thoughts. *I really should tell him I won't be around in two weeks*, I thought; but I pushed aside the whole move thing as my car service pulled into the pick-up lane.

I'd tell him later—as soon as I figured out how.

"Talk to Winter," I said, "and then call me this weekend." And without really thinking about it, I kissed Micah good-bye.

He stood there for a moment, stunned, before he grinned his little Micah grin and stepped on his skateboard, pushing off with a burst of energy.

I felt pretty glossy. I still hadn't come up with a new word.

20

Tech Support

The *step-whir* in my head beat out a rhythm like the wings of rabid hummingbirds as I watched Micah and Nora get into Officer Bell's car.

My *sasuke-san* put his hand on my shoulder. "They'll be fine," he said. "Bell just wants to talk to them."

I trusted my grandfather's judgment, but I still felt jittery watching my best friend (and his girl) pull away in the backseat of a police car. Maybe it was just the bad coffee making me feel that way. The hummingbirds didn't think so.

"Let's go home," Grandfather said. He gave me a quick hug.

We walked down the alley to Jefferson Street. We didn't say much. I was still sorting out the questions flitting through my head. We stopped at the bus stop in front of Starbucks. We've been busing it for years, ever since Grandfather's car was blown up outside his shop. It had happened not long after Mom and Dad disappeared. Since Grandfather didn't have insurance, he'd never replaced the car. He inclined his head in the direction of the baristas serving up reasonably good coffee. I shook my head.

"That's a first," he said.

"Grandfather?" I started to ask him the question that had floated to the top of my brain, but the number 72 bus picked that moment to turn the corner and grind to a halt in front of us.

We grabbed seats toward the front. It wasn't a long ride to our place. I could wait to ask him then. An ad for some cologne I'd never heard of was playing; but as soon as our butts hit the vinyl, the screen flicked over to the news. I had to smile. I think we confuse the system. We don't buy much from retail markets, and not many vintage shops or tattoo parlors can afford to advertise on public transport. Most of the time I get Nomura products or the news. Grandfather usually gets cars. Guess the system thinks he needs a new one.

The local reporter woman was interviewing a new candidate for the senate outside a TFC downtown. "I never forget who I represent," he said with a gleaming smile.

Grandfather groaned. "TFC is sponsoring him," he explained without looking away from his mobile. "Nomura is being stingy with its funds this time around, which probably means your uncle doesn't like this guy too much.

Ichiro will let TFC or one of its flunkies, like Soft Target or Homeland Inc., foot the bill for this guy."

Politics, family or otherwise, bores me; but the reporter looked familiar. Then it clicked. "That's where I've seen her," I said to no one in particular. "That's Jet's girlfriend."

Grandfather looked up at the screen. "Yeah, that's Becca. Jet's been working on her back piece for a few months now."

Rebecca Starr is cute, a bit more boyish than I like. Jet is curvier. Wait. *Becca?* That meant he knows her pretty well.

"They moved in together," Grandfather said gently, as if he knew how I felt about Jet. I'd never told anyone about my crush on Jet, except Velvet—and she guessed. "They seem really happy."

Shit.

"Eighth and Day," the bus announced as it jerked to a stop.

Thank God. I couldn't get off of the bus fast enough. I did not want to hear Grandfather say that I'll meet someone someday or some crap like that. He didn't, but he seemed a little too aware of my discomfort as we walked toward our place.

Question time.

"Why is your group so threatened by a stupid comic strip drawn by a couple of kids?"

That wiped the grin off his face. He retina-scanned us into our front entrance. The big door slid shut behind us, and the security system beeped to indicate the place was locked—and bug free. A customer had installed this quasi-legal anti-surveillance system for us a few years ago in exchange for a full-body piece. Grandfather had felt we needed the security because of what had happened to my folks. He's still working on that tattoo.

"It's true that the Jonas Fund could get us all in hot water," he said as he grabbed juice from the fridge. "And some people, like Katie, think it's our most important function, and we shouldn't be doing anything that could screw it up. But I think most of the group is nervous because of the black vans."

"Micah drew them in *Memento*." I shook my head when Grandfather offered me a glass of juice. I hopped onto the counter over the recycling unit.

He nodded. "We've been watching the vans for a while—Bell and I—and we think they're connected to incidents that happen later. Car bombings, mostly. So *Memento* might attract the wrong kind of attention for the group. You're my granddaughter, and you're giving out the comic at Doug and Katie's school."

"Wait. Vans? You mean the Coalition is using the black vans to blow up stuff? Then why don't you guys report it? You don't support what the Coalition does, right?"

Grandfather looked at me like I was five. Of course, Grandfather would never support the Coalition. And he, Bell, and everyone else would be heroes if they turned in any information about the bombings. I realized I'd been kicking the metal door of the recycling unit and stopped.

"You mean it's not the Coalition?"

He shrugged. "Some people think the Coalition might not be behind everything that blows up these days."

The hummingbirds beat their wings into a frenzy. It was almost as hard to think as when I took my meds. I think I started tapping my foot again, but it couldn't keep up with the hummingbirds. Finally I got a word out. "Explain."

"All of the attacks in the beginning—the World Trade Center, the London tube, that train in Madrid—were all done by various terrorist groups for different reasons. Separate, unconnected incidents. Then it was quiet for many years, at least outside the Middle East. Until that plane took out the bridge in San Francisco about the time you were born. At first there was some debate over whether it was really a terrorist act or just a terrible accident, but a new group calling itself the Coalition took credit for it. Afterward, smaller things started happening more and more often across the country until it was almost a daily occurrence." Grandfather stilled my foot with his. "Everything since the Golden Gate has been blamed on the quote-unquote Coalition."

"But if you don't believe it's the Coalition, then who do you think is really doing it?"

"Certain corporate interests."

"What about the government? Why would they let this go on?"

"Governments, corporations—same thing. One owns the

other, right? And business is booming." Grandfather wasn't laughing. "Scared people are good citizen-consumers." He let that sink in. "I know. It's hard to believe and nearly impossible to prove. A lot of people have disappeared trying to do so—or because they stumbled onto something. A whole watch group in South Florida vanished a few months ago. Which is why the MLSG doesn't want you involved."

"Afraid we'll mess it up and blow their cover, huh?"

"They don't want anything to happen to you." He drained his glass. "Or themselves," he added with a wink.

"What do *you* want, Ojiisan?" I hopped down from the counter and stood in front of him.

"I don't want to lose you, too." His voice caught as he said it. He put his hand over his heart, over the snowflake he'd tattooed there for me fourteen and a half years ago.

"I'm just the tech support." This time I winked.

He didn't look convinced. "Don't think so little of yourself or your friends," he said. "But be careful."

"Me? You're the one chasing black vans." All this time I'd thought he was just patrolling the neighborhood, looking for burglars and muggers.

The hummingbirds were making an unbearable racket in my head. "I need to tinker."

"And I need to work out," he said. He kissed me on the forehead before he disappeared.

I walked through the garden to my workshop.

Did I underestimate my friends? I had to admit Nora had *huevos*. She laid out her story there and stood up to the

MLSG, but I wasn't completely sure she was my friend—or Micah's. He was the one I worried about. He had no one. Just his mom and a few other homeless people looking out for him. He was the one who would go down hard for this if it went bad.

And I knew it would. The hummingbirds told me.

I had to finish my garden.

21

I Can Still Smell the Fruit Loops

Therapeutic Statement *42-03282028-12*
Subject: *WALLENBERG, MICAH JONAS, 15*
Facility: *HAMILTON DETENTION CENTER TFC-42*

She kissed me. Again. That was the only thing going through my brain, like a loop playing over and over again, as I pushed off toward home. That and the smell of her hair. Like Fruit Loops. I love Fruit Loops. We don't get those too often in the Village. My board glided over the ramps and sidewalks and handrails until I got to the King footbridge.

I wasn't quite ready to go home yet. I plopped myself down by the statue. From there you can see the back end of downtown—the reverse of the skyline you see on the city logo—with Memorial Avenue running right through it.

My brain wandered off from the Fruit Loops to darker areas, like cops and black vans. I, for one, was looking forward to some ride-along action with the Black Van Committee, but I didn't know how I was going to stand not knowing until then. At least I'd get to see Nora on Monday. And she definitely said to call her this weekend.

I got out my sketch pad, cranked up the tunes on my mobile—a little Lo-Fi Strangers I'd cadged off Spike. I started out drawing Nora; but as my mind went to that chill, kind of glossy-in-a-good-way place it goes when I draw, I began sketching black vans and crowds of people. I could see where my story and the cop's intersected.

I poured it out on paper, not all of it, just a scene or two, while the Strangers croaked out "My credit rating sucks and so do you" through my earbuds.

The lights on the bridge started to flicker on as the sun dipped behind the copper roof of the Alexander Hamilton Building. I was losing my light, so I watched the traffic roll down Memorial for a few minutes. Most of it was buses or car services—you can tell by the armor plating—fleeing from the city center. All except this black van streaking toward downtown. I stuffed everything into my bag and hopped on my board and rode it down the handi-ramp to the street. The van was long gone now. A cop car coming the other way slowed. Its blackened window slid down as it pulled up alongside me.

"Unless you have a work or sports permit, you better get home, kid," the cop said. Her Homeland Inc. badge flashed Jacinda W. "The eighteen-and-under curfew starts in twenty," she added, not waiting for me to reply. Without a pass or an adult, no kids can be on the street after dark in our fair metropolis. She hit her flashers and took off after a speeding limo.

"On my way, officer," I said to the back of her car.

• • •

Mrs. Brooks scolded me for being late again, but she'd saved me a big bowl of excellent vegetarian chili and a hunk of sunflower fennel French bread. Mom was working another double. She's determined to get us our own apartment again by Christmas. Most places these days require a wad of cash up front if you have a shit security score like we do. First three months' rent. Last three. Security deposits. Cleaning fees. Credit check. Security check. I'd rather just stay in Black Dog Village, but I get it. Mom wants us to have our own place. How could I get mad at her for that? Especially since I keep screwing up and costing her money. I know the emergency room isn't free. We can't afford insurance.

Mrs. Brooks sank into the seat next to me with a big cup of coffee in one of her new blue-glazed cups. She asked me how my day was, and I nearly choked on my bread.

"Chew, boy," she said. She looked real tired, and I knew that wasn't decaf in her cup. She volunteers at a soup kitchen twice a week on top of everything she does here.

"Mrs. Brooks, have you heard anything about black vans?" I asked. She knows a lot of people—on the streets and off. Church people. Cops. Delivery drivers. People more homeless than us.

She looked at me hard. "Young man, you steer clear of any unmarked black vehicles you see in this city. Or any city." There wasn't a hint of that stern-but-not-really thing in her voice. She was dead serious. "Why do you ask?"

"No reason," I said, and then chewed furiously. Mom hadn't told anyone in Black Dog how I'd broken my arm. I guess they all assumed I'd wiped out on my board. "Just had a dream about one hitting me," I added when I could see she wasn't buying it. It wasn't exactly a lie. I had that dream sometimes. And sometimes a bunch of apes in football jerseys drove the van.

I probably could have told her about the whole memory support group run-in and about *Memento*, but Mrs. Brooks might tell Mom. And then she'd figure out I never took the pill. That would really freak her out.

I fetched the rest of the firewood for Mrs. B. before I hit the sack, but I couldn't really sleep. I pulled on my jeans and padded out barefoot to the playground. Here you didn't have to worry about junkies and terrorists when you couldn't sleep. Melinda Peterson waved to me as she sat in front of her cottage having a late-night smoke and a cup of herbal tea. She usually waits up for her husband to come home from his job scrubbing floors at the courthouse. I sat atop the jungle gym and stared at the stars for a while. The city slept. I could still feel Nora's lips on mine. And I could still smell the Fruit Loops.

In the quiet, I heard the distinct sound of a car bomb going off somewhere. Maybe uptown.

That's when it clicked in my head. Black vans. Car bombs. Duh. Crazy, but so duh that no one would believe it.

22

I Disappoint My Father

Therapeutic Statement 42-03282028-11
Subject: JAMES, NORA EMILY, 15
Facility: HAMILTON DETENTION CENTER TFC-42

Sliding into the backseat of the car, I was still feeling pretty glossy from that kiss—until I bumped right into Dad.

"Well, now I know what you were doing," he said as he rifled through some papers in his briefcase. An ad played across the bulletproof screen between the driver and us. "I thought I'd surprise you by picking you up after my meeting with your principal. Thought I might treat you to a slice of pizza or something with your old man. Imagine my surprise—and *worry*—when I find the library's closed and you're not answering your mobile." He still didn't look at me. I had noticed the missed calls when I buzzed the car service, but my brain had been otherwise occupied.

I knew I had to say something—fast—but I was totally

not used to lying to my father. Not telling him things, yes, but not outright lying.

On the screen, purple mountains faded into a boardroom and then into a little girl blowing on a dandelion; the barest hint of a flag waved underneath everything like a ghost. *Securing our way of life*, the final frame said. *Soft Target*.

"Uh, yeah, the librarian had to leave early so we went to the art studio," I said. "And I left my mobile in my locker." At least the last part was true.

"Uh-huh." He kept staring at the piece of paper in his hand. What was it? That actually concerned me more than him thinking I was making out with Micah. I didn't think I'd flunked anything, and Officer Bell obviously hadn't told the principal what he knew.

"Why were you meeting with the principal, Dad?" I asked.

"You saw this, didn't you?" he said, handing me the latest issue of *Memento*.

The temperature in the car felt as if it were about a hundred degrees.

"Everyone did," I managed to say.

"I know. It got all over town. Other cities, too, but we've determined it started here. My client isn't happy."

I wondered which client would care about an underground comic drawn by a few high school kids. I mean, Homeland Inc. would. It was their school, but Dad had never mentioned working for them before. It wasn't like I knew his whole client list, though.

He looked up from the paper at me. "Your principal doesn't have any proof, but she thinks one young Micah Wallenberg, your new boyfriend, is the only one in this school talented enough to draw this. Or this." He pulled out a copy of the first issue from a plain brown folder. "Interesting story line, don't you think?"

I waited for him to say something. Anything. When he didn't, I knew.

He knew. Everything.

He held his lighter under the comic and watched the flames lick the paper for a moment. Then he threw the last bits of it out the window just as we turned down the street.

"You've disappointed me, daughter." He looked at me, his expression softer, sadder. "I thought you were smarter than that. You may think this is just a harmless flirtation with a rebellious bad boy—but you'll get hurt. And I, for one, don't want that. I want you to get into a good school, carve out a nice career for yourself, meet the *right* kind of young man, and be happy."

I could tell he really meant what he said.

I didn't say anything. Even though I believed in *Memento*, I still felt as if I'd let him down.

"Give me your mobile," he said.

I handed him my Pink Ice. He pressed a couple of digits on his mobile and handed mine back to me. I knew what he'd done without looking. He'd cut me off from everything except homework and his or Mom's calls. He didn't need to do all that in front of me—he could have done it from anywhere, anytime—but he wanted me to watch.

"You're not to see that boy again. In fact, you're grounded until we move. And then you're restricted to the compound indefinitely."

He let me out in front of our house.

After I closed the car door the car window slid down.

"Nora, I'm going to have a long talk with your mother about this when I get home," he said. And then the car took off.

I knew how those long talks ended.

I raced inside to warn Mom. I found her sitting on the kitchen floor, cleaning out the cabinets, a big box marked SMALL APPLIANCES by her side.

"You—we—we need to leave now before Dad gets home," I told her.

"What?" She put a mixer I'd never seen her use in the box.

"We have to go *now*," I implored. I grabbed her mobile off the counter and tossed it to her.

"Calm down, Nora. What's wrong?" She taped up the box with maddening calmness.

I took a deep breath. The important thing was to get her out of the house. I could explain it all later. "I did something Dad didn't like. And he said he'd 'talk' to you about it." As soon as the words came out of my mouth, I realized how ridiculous they sounded.

"Nora Emily James! What did you do?" Mom scrambled up off the floor.

This was not going the way I wanted. She wasn't going to budge unless I told her something. Should I tell her I spit out the pill? That I remembered what she'd forgotten? That I put out an underground comic about it? That I just rode home with a cop from a meeting of people Dad would call terrorists?

"Well?"

I opted for the safest version. "I've been hanging out with this boy Dad doesn't like." That sounded so stupid.

"Is that all?" Mom was relieved, but then she asked, "You two haven't been doing anything? You're not pregnant, are you?"

"It's not like that at all," I insisted. *As if*.

"Nora, do you really like this boy?"

"That's so not the point, Mom." How could I get it through her glossy head that Dad was dangerous?

"Honey, don't worry. If you really like him, we could have him over for dinner, and your Dad will come around. I'll talk to him." She put her arm around me.

"No!" I squirmed free. That's exactly what I didn't want her to do. Talk to him.

"And why not?"

I was going to have to say it. "Things happen when you two talk. He hits you." I said the last part quietly.

"Don't be ridiculous!" She was pissed.

But I had to keep going. "That's why you go to TFC. To forget." She must know that, somewhere inside.

"Enough, young lady! I will not listen to another word. Go to your room." Mom turned her back on me and started packing again.

"But, Mom—"

"Enough."

◾ ◾ ◾

I heard the argument that night as I was lying in bed. He was more convinced than ever that moving to Los Palamos was the right thing to do. And that I needed to be kept away from "certain elements." And that it was all her fault for not keeping a better eye on me. I heard her protest.

Again I thought, *How could I have not heard this racket before?*

I knew they fought. But everyone's parents fight. I remembered some raised voices every once in a while. Dad had always said it was over dumb stuff. He worked too late. She spent too much. It was his turn to take out the garbage. He'd tell me all about it when he brought me a cup of cocoa before bed. Then he'd say, "Drink up, Princess, and tell me every little thing that's bothering you. Don't leave anything out." I'd always loved when he said that. And I'd tell him everything while I sipped that hot chocolate dotted with red cinnamon sprinkles and his "secret ingredient." It tasted like nutmeg, but I let him pretend it was a mystery. In the morning I always felt so glossy.

It hit me then. That's why I didn't remember.

Dad's biggest client is TFC. His secret ingredient isn't nutmeg. And I'd reactivated the memory of each fight (and who knows what else?) when I told him "every little thing."

Only, after the bombing, I'd been the sulky teenager rather than his little princess. Good-bye, cocoa. Hello, TFC.

I suddenly felt so cold. And so alone. I pulled the covers over my head and tried really, really hard not to hear the yelling.

I lay awake long after they were done. A door closed somewhere in the house, and it was silent. I listened for the sound of flip-flops making their way down the hall, for the clink of a cup and saucer coming toward my room.

They didn't come. I knew they wouldn't, but in a weird way I hoped I could go back in time.

I wished Micah were here.

*   *   *

In the morning Mom had a cast on her wrist. Fresh flowers sat on the countertop. And she wanted me to go to TFC.

"I'm fine," I insisted. Neither of us were able to look the other in the eye.

All of a sudden I was angry. At her. "Anyway, I'm grounded. Remember?" I hurled the words at her like a kitchen knife. Then I stomped back upstairs and slammed my door.

I wanted to spend the rest of the weekend holed up in my room, letting them think I was brooding about being grounded. I couldn't. I felt bad about being angry with Mom. And about being the cause of her latest "accident."

I found her packing up the dining room. Dad was out playing golf with clients. She was fumbling with a wine glass, her wrist making it hard to wrap the stem in bubble wrap. I caught the glass as it slipped from her hands.

"Thanks." She sniffled. She'd clearly been crying. Now I felt really bad.

"Sorry," I said, picking up another glass to wrap.

Mom didn't say anything. We just packed in silence for a while. The cast on her wrist, however, was a constant reminder to me of what we weren't talking about. I sealed one box and set it on the floor.

I had to try once more. "Why don't you leave him? Or at least tell him you don't want to move."

Mom looked at me strangely. "Why would I want to leave him? He didn't mean it. This was an accident." She held up her wrist. "I'm certainly not happy about the move, but sometimes you have to make sacrifices for the ones you love."

That's when I finally gave up.

*   *   *

On Monday morning I made a promise to myself: I wouldn't even glance at Micah or Winter in school.

23

Ditched

Therapeutic Statement 42-03282028-12
Subject: WALLENBERG, MICAH JONAS, 15
Facility: HAMILTON DETENTION CENTER TFC-42

She totally blew me off. All day. I waved to her in the hallway, and she ducked into the bathroom. I waited for her after English class; her friends materialized out of fricking nowhere to whisk her off to lunch. I casually looked in her direction in the caf and that preppie-jock-douche-bag Tom Slayton stared me down like a Rottweiler guarding a bone. I couldn't even send her a message. Every time I did, a perky synthetic voice said, "We're sorry. This user is not accepting calls from you at this time."

I got it. She wanted to keep us on the down-low. She has an image to maintain.

I should have told Nora to go to hell. But I didn't. I wanted to tell her about my van theory. I wanted to keep doing *Memento*. And I just wanted to be with her. *I am such a loser*.

The only thing that brightened my day was the Senior Prank. They'd papered all the ad screens in the school—on the lockers, in the classrooms, in the hallways—with what looked like blank paper. But if you got really close—like, say, too close for the surveillance cams to focus on—you could see that each piece of paper had a tiny letter on it. An M on this one. An E on the next, and so on. They spelled out *MEMENTO*. It was freaking brilliant.

As the last bell rang for the day, I pushed open the library door, nodded to Ms. Curtis behind the counter, and then slumped into our usual spot. I got out my sketch pad and waited. And waited. My mobile said it was four. Maybe she couldn't duck her friends. Five more minutes.

I heard Ms. Curtis clear her throat, and I dived into one of the books on the top of the pile. Ms. Curtis slid a new art book across the table. *Edward Hopper*. On the cover was his famous painting of people sitting in a diner late at night. No one is talking. Everyone is alone—the couple, the guy behind the counter, the guy with his back to us. Alone.

"It's a new edition. Just came in," Ms. Curtis said.

I could smell its newness as I flipped through the clean pages. Ms. Curtis was still standing there. "Thanks," I said, and kept flipping through the book, hoping she'd go away. She didn't.

"You know, Micah, it's difficult for Nora," she said.

I took a good look at the librarian, maybe for the first time ever. I bet she was the cute, rich, popular girl once. She might have been Nora twenty years ago. I wondered who she'd lost before joining the MLSG.

"She might think she's doing the best thing for both of you," Ms. Curtis said.

Crap. Even the librarian knew it. Nora ditched me for real.

I shut the Hopper book. "You mean best for *her*." I grabbed my bag and board and booked it out of there. No pun intended.

Outside, I dropped my board to the sidewalk and kicked. I didn't know where I was going, but in the back of my head I held on to the hope that Nora hadn't totally given up on us. Or *Memento*.

24

Bad Digits

Therapeutic Statement 42-03282028-13
Subject: NOMURA, WINTER, 14
Facility: HAMILTON DETENTION CENTER TFC-42

Gears. That's what it is all about. Wheels upon wheels making shit turn. A system. All the good sprockets, big and small, going in the same direction, whether they wanted to or not. If one breaks, replace it with a shiny new one. At least that's what the little whirring hummingbird inside my head was telling me.

I'd pulled gears out of every piece of junk I could lay my hands on, and it still wasn't enough. Most things now have only ones and zeroes spinning around in a hunk of plastic. No metal teeth gnashing, turning each other, making things work. Like clockwork. In a digital system, all you have to do is erase the bad digit and go on like nothing ever happened.

I couldn't have an even number of gears. That wouldn't work. Needed to be odd. A prime number would be really glossy. Ugh. I hate that word. Brilliant. A prime number would be brilliant. Seventeen gears from the eye to the drum, from this one the size of a dime to the big, red, dinner plate–sized one.

I laid out all my scrounged and pilfered gears on the table in my gazebo. It was a jigsaw puzzle with missing pieces, ones I'd have to make myself. I could see it all turning in my head. A big pot of coffee steamed on the side table. My solar sails tinkled gently in the moonlight. I was ready to get this done. And Grandfather was scarce. He knew to leave me alone when I was like this.

So, of course, Micah burst into the garden from the back gate. He was talking so fast, even I couldn't follow him. It totally crushed my manic high. I might as well have taken my meds.

He was all *Is she here? Why is she doing this? What did I do?*

"Chill," I told him. I laughed because, for once, it was me doing the chilling.

He'd floated over Saturday evening all happy and shit to share what Bell had told him and Nora and how he'd come up with this theory that maybe it wasn't the Coalition after all. It matched what Grandfather had told me on our way home.

"Is she here?" Micah asked again, more calmly this time.

Obviously he meant Nora. Lover boy wasn't so happy anymore. She'd been icing him out since Friday. He'd called her a hundred times. Nada. Clearly he'd hoped she'd still show today.

"What did you do to her?" I asked.

"Kissed her," he said. "Well, she kissed me," he back-pedaled.

There you go. I'd wondered how long it would take for her to revert to type. And her type doesn't date ours. Even if they were cool enough to get involved with Micah in the first place.

"She's not like that," he said, although I hadn't said anything out loud.

Yeah? What's she like? I didn't say that out loud, either. I just thought it real hard as I stared at him, searching for whatever gear inside of him was grinding itself to bits over this girl.

"Cut it out," he said. "Where are Bell and your grand-dad?"

Of course, tonight was that stupid ride-along with Sasuke-san's posse of black-van stalkers. I didn't want to go. I didn't want Grandfather to go. And I was hoping Micah would blow it off—like he always does when he loses interest in something, which he always does. He's always on to something new and more interesting, like welding or comic books or graffiti or girls. Always.

I groaned. That pissed him off.

"Don't you give a shit about anything?" he asked.

That wasn't fair. I turned my back on him. I'm not the one who didn't show up, wouldn't return his calls, wouldn't even look at him in school.

"I give a shit about this," I said, tossing a gear on the table. "And I wish people would just leave me alone and let me finish it."

"Fine. I'll leave you alone with your crap," he said. "I'm going with Mr. Yamada and Bell."

"No, you aren't." It was Grandfather. Officer Bell stood behind him, with this sorry-kids look on his face. "You're not coming with us. Either of you. Micah, go home or stay here tonight."

"But—" Micah shut up when he looked at Grandfather.

Bell just shrugged. "He's right, kid," he told Micah. "It's too dangerous tonight. I heard on the police frequency that they're doing a bum sweep of sector six, which is usually a bad sign."

"*Bum* sweep?" Micah asked. He pronounced the first word as if it hurt him.

Officer Bell didn't notice. "Yeah, we, the police, pick them up," Bell explained. "I heard there was a sweep before the Market Street bombing a few weeks ago."

"Are you saying you cops *know* when there's going to be a bombing?" I asked. A fierce little hummingbird reminded me that the cops are owned by one of the biggest companies in the U.S.: Homeland Inc.

"Not exactly," Bell said. "We just get told to clear an area—and stay out of it for a while. Then shit happens."

"Who exactly is doing this *shit*?" Micah asked. "No, wait. Let *me* tell *you*."

Micah explained his theory: the so-called Coalition doesn't exist. It's really some secret corporate-government cabal bent on keeping the people scared.

Grandfather nodded. "We think the black vans are operated by a contractor here in Hamilton."

"But we don't have any proof," Bell quickly added.

"A contractor? You mean someone working for the government, right?" Micah asked.

"Or a bigger corporation," I said. "Who, in turn, might be working for the government." *Or vice versa. Gears turning gears*, the hummingbird told me.

"We don't know," Bell admitted lamely. He suspected, though. I could see it in the way he chewed the inside of his cheek. He just couldn't prove it. "A reporter in Philly was investigating the connection last year, but she disappeared just before the story was supposed to be 'cast. It's no coincidence that TFC owns a lot of the newscasts."

"Stay here," Grandfather said, looking from me to Micah.

I glared at him, and he knew exactly what I was thinking. "We'll be okay, Win-chan. We have Bell's police radio and a few other tricks up our sleeve," he said as he pulled on his half-fingered gloves.

All of a sudden I had a vision of my grandfather climbing fire escapes and pulling himself along ledges, just like he trained for on his Sasuke course. *Game show, my ass.*

Micah stood there, holding his skateboard in his good hand as if he was weighing his options. "Okay," he finally said.

Grandfather and Bell left. Micah dropped his board to the ground and turned to me without saying anything. He didn't need to.

"Go," I said. *Keep an eye on my ojiisan*, I silently commanded him.

Micah pushed off, wheels spinning faster than the gears in my head.

*   *   *

Later Micah texted me to have the printer ready tomorrow night. He just had to see her first.

Idiot, I replied.

But that's when it all came together in my head. That's when I saw what those gears needed to do.

I didn't sleep at all that night.

25

Life's Better in a Chevy

Therapeutic Statement 42-03282028-12
Subject: WALLENBERG, MICAH JONAS, 15
Facility: HAMILTON DETENTION CENTER TFC-42

I'm glad Nora didn't come, I told myself as I rolled down the alley behind the Nomuras' place. I pulled my black hoodie tight around my face. I knew she never had my back, at least not out here. Nora'd never lived on the streets; she'd never even been out after curfew. Okay, Mom and I were never technically on the streets. But I used to roam around while Mom worked nights. You could only lie under the blankets in the backseat of a ten-year-old Chevy Fresno ignoring your homework and listening to the same tunes for so long. I got mugged once; that was enough for those guys to figure out I had less than they did.

I followed Bell's gray, unmarked police car as it pulled out of the garage. I could see the silhouette of him and Mr. Yamada. I followed them on my board for a couple blocks, careful to keep to the shadows and out of the security cams. Then they turned right onto Market. By the time I got to the corner, they were out of sight. They could've turned down any cross street. No one was on the streets at this hour. Almost no one.

I ducked into a doorway as another car turned onto Market. A black-and-white police car. It flashed by without noticing me.

I had no idea where Bell was going or where sector 6 was. I could go back to Winter's. Or go home. I needed to know for sure, though, that the vans were doing what we thought they were doing. I mean, it was crazy. And what if we put that idea in the comic strip and it was wrong? What if it was right and we did nothing? Then I remembered something Bell had said. Something I'd already drawn. He'd said he'd followed the van back to a parking structure next to Tiffany's. I knew where that was.

I pointed my board in the direction of the jewelry store by way of a couple of alleys and pushed off hard. Maybe I could catch a van coming out of the garage. If I got lucky. Really lucky.

But I never made it to Tiffany's or the parking structure. As I was skating down the alley between Eighteenth and Central, I saw a black van creep past the end of the alley. I hugged the wall until it passed. Then I skated like hell to get to the end of the alley. From there I could see it cruising very slowly down Eighteenth, as if it was looking for something. Or like a patrol car does when it's checking out the neighborhood, searching for curfew breakers and thugs. The van turned left onto the next street. I dashed across Eighteenth and headed down the alley parallel to the van.

I skated hard. I wanted to beat the van to Nineteenth Street so I'd know which way it went. I slalomed around some dumpsters, and the smell of warm garbage and piss brought back memories of creeping around like this while Mom worked.

Suddenly a dark figure swung down from a fire escape. I swerved and clotheslined the guy with my cast. I could hear the plaster crack and the *oomph* of someone hitting the pavement as I kicked off hard. I'd thought it had been a little too quiet out. In the old days I'd always see someone dumpster diving for dinner or curled up in a box sleeping in the alley.

"Micah," a familiar voice called. It was Mr. Yamada. Not exactly who I'd expected to meet in a dark alley.

I stopped. "Dude." I fumbled for words. "What are you doing here?" I knew what he was doing there in general, but I hadn't expected him to come swinging down a fire escape at me. I'd imagined him and Bell cozy in the gray cop car doing the stakeout thing. "Are you okay?" I skated back toward him.

Mr. Yamada stood up.

"Damn, kiddo, I should know better than to ninja up on a skater boy," he said, rubbing his chin and grinning.

"I'm sorry," I said. I felt bad for hitting him, an old man and all, but we didn't have time for this. "There's a van creeping around the block right now."

The smile evaporated from his face. He scrambled back up the outside of the fire escape and onto the roof in one fluid motion—like a spider monkey. Then I heard the crackle of a walkie-talkie, like the ones they use in old war movies, coming from the top of the roof. Mr. Yamada must have spotted the van.

I raced down the alley. I could see the van idling a couple of blocks down Nineteenth—by a parked car on the opposite side of the street. Carrying my board, I ran half crouching through the shadows to a doorway about a block from the van.

I saw a guy in a dark uniform of some sort; I couldn't see any markings, but it didn't look like cop or military issue. He had on gloves and a watch cap, though it was pretty warm out. The guy—at least I think it was a guy—put something in the wheel well above the front driver side tire. He slapped a sticker on the front windshield and then jumped into the back of the van as it peeled away. The whole operation took just seconds.

As I crept down the block, I saw another car pull slowly up to the opposite corner. It stopped about twenty-five yards away. It was Bell. I heard the walkie-talkie crackle again as he rolled down his window.

I picked up my board and ran commando style over to Bell's car. I rapped on the window.

"Jesus, kid, you scared me," Bell said as he rolled his window down farther. "You need to get out of here now."

"Did they do what I think they did?" I asked.

"Get in," he said.

Mr. Yamada ran up to the passenger side.

"What are you going to do about this?" I asked them, still not getting in. "What if someone tries to drive the car? Did you check to see if anyone is sleeping in there now?"

"They slapped a shutdown sticker on the vehicle. It can't be driven," Bell explained rather casually. "Well, most of the time. Besides, who in their right mind would be sleeping in a car these days?"

Crap, I thought. It would take too long to explain. I skated over to the car, which was an old beater, a yellow Chevy a lot like my mom's old car. Lights were on in the building behind it. I circled around and peeked in the back. There was a lumpy pile of blankets and clothes across the seat, and I heard the faint sounds of the *Haji Patrol* theme song coming from underneath. I tapped on the window, and the sound cut out. I tapped again.

"Dude, get up," I said. "Someone's been messing with your car. You could be toast in a few minutes."

A kid's head popped up and looked at me in a panic. He couldn't have been more than twelve. And he didn't know whether I was waiting to jack his gear or was telling the truth. I backed away from the car.

I waved off Mr. Yamada and supercop as they came running at the car. Nothing would scare the kid more than a couple guys in black rushing his crib.

"Dude, no lie. I saw some guy put something under the driver side. Ease out toward me."

He still didn't move.

"Is your mom working in this building?" I asked, pointing behind me. "Cleaning or something?"

He nodded.

"Better go warn her. You don't want her to get hurt," I said, and backed off even farther.

The kid climbed out of the car slowly in his camo pj's and bare feet, his mobile clutched in his hand. He looked from me to Bell to Mr. Yamada.

"This dude's a cop." I pointed to Bell, who had the sense to flash his badge. "He can get you and your mom to somewhere safe."

The kid rabbited into the building. Bell followed.

Mr. Yamada looked at me. Then he bowed and offered to bring me home.

"Nah, I'm okay," I said. "Take care of those people who almost got blown up." I pushed off toward home before he could say anything else.

I wasn't really okay, though. Six months ago that could have been me. I shivered as I wound through the alleys and side streets toward Black Dog Village.

I got about a half mile away before the explosion went off.

26

Behind the Gates

Therapeutic Statement 42-03282028-11
Subject: JAMES, NORA EMILY, 15
Facility: HAMILTON DETENTION CENTER TFC-42

I successfully avoided Micah for a whole seventy-two hours, not counting the weekend. My girls ran interference for me at school. They assumed I was finally nipping an undesirable relationship in the bud. And when the girls weren't around, I ducked into the bathroom and other places when I saw him coming.

Monday, I darted into the library without thinking. Then I realized he was going to follow me. It was kind of our place. But Ms. Curtis instantly understood the situation. She hid me in her office.

"You're doing the right thing," she said as she squeezed one of those stress thingies she keeps on her desk. "Sometimes you've got to do unpleasant things to protect the ones you love. Things they might not like you for."

For a second I thought that Ms. Curtis knew about my mom somehow. Then I realized she was talking about Micah. She meant I was protecting him by ditching him. And I guess I was.

"I don't know about *love*," I said. But I did feel better about what I was doing. "Thanks. Tell the group *Memento* is history." Just like Micah and me.

"Good." She released the stress ball and let it drop onto her desk.

I still didn't understand why the group cared, why she cared. As the pink ball rolled toward me, I could see it had the *Behind the Gates* logo on it. I felt a weird kinship with her.

"Who did you lose?" I asked.

"Pardon?"

"You said the people who'd started the group had all lost someone to you-know-where."

"My mother." That's all she said.

"Oh." I don't know what I'd expected, a brother or boyfriend maybe. Winter's mom was in the Big D, so I shouldn't have been surprised. But I was.

Ms. Curtis didn't look like she wanted to discuss her mom, but I had a crazy urge to talk to her about mine. "Can I tell you something?"

She nodded, and the whole thing about my parents spilled out of my mouth. How he beat her. How she forgot it. How he'd told me to stop seeing Micah. The only thing I left out was the cocoa. It felt good, but as soon as it was all out of my mouth, I worried that Ms. Curtis would have to report it to someone. So I asked her, just to be sure.

"Technically, I only have to report *child* abuse." She looked me in the eye, I guess checking to see if I were lying and my dad was hitting me, too. "I know you've been through a lot, Nora." She was silent for a moment. "Your secret is safe with me," she finally said, shaking her head slightly. "But please know you can come to me if things get worse or if you need anything. Anything at all." I noticed she'd picked up the stress ball again while I was talking and was rolling it around in her hands.

"Thanks," I said, relieved.

She nodded. "You're doing the right thing."

I felt better, and I didn't.

My mobile buzzed, and I dashed out the door.

• • •

The next day when Micah approached our table at lunch, I let Tom Slayton, egged on by the girls, stare down Micah and tell him to piss off. But I ached to talk to him. Micah, not Tom. And Tom took the whole situation as a sign. An invitation. Maybe the girls clued him in. He walked me to my next class. And he was waiting there when it was over. And he even asked me to the prom. I told him I'd love to but I was indefinitely grounded. I never mentioned we'd probably be "behind the gates" of Los Palamos by then. I still hadn't told anyone about the move.

The girls were thrilled with the Tom Slayton development. He's so Stone Collins, Abby said. Very glossy, Maia agreed. I could feel Winter looking through me when I passed her in the hall, as if she could see how hollow I really was.

Dad would probably approve of Tom Slayton, too, I thought as Tom walked me to history class. He was talking about which colleges had the best pre-law programs and lacrosse teams. But the thought of living behind the gates with a Tom Slayton was so dreary, I wanted to cry. I told him I'd see him later and ran into the bathroom.

In there, a junior girl I didn't know asked me to sign a petition to bring back the school newspaper. We used to have one, she explained, back when her big brother went here.

"Homeland blamed it on budget cuts," she said, rolling her eyes as she handed me the clipboard, "but we all know they just didn't 'approve' of what we had to say." She already had 283 signatures.

While I was signing, an announcement played on the ad screen over the sink. Senior Skip Day had been canceled because of the prank.

"Typical," the girl said on her way out.

*　*　*

Wednesday was a lot of the same. But that evening our home security system announced a visitor, and then someone knocked on the door to my room. I prayed that it wouldn't be Tom.

It wasn't. It was Micah.

"You okay? I told your mom I needed your help on our art history project," Micah said, pulling his sketchbook out of his trusty messenger bag.

I didn't say anything. I just sat on the bed like a lump.

"What's wrong?" he asked. "I was worried when you didn't show at Winter's. When you didn't answer your messages. When you let that jock-head blow me off yesterday," he said, hurt. He took a few steps closer.

"I can't do it anymore," I told him. I pulled my knees up to my chin and wrapped my arms around them.

"Wait," he said, pulling something from his sketchbook. "Before you make up your mind, look at this."

He spread the next issue of *Memento*, minus the words, on the bed in front of me. Then he stepped back.

The first half I recognized. It was the cop's story. Black vans and all.

"I did a little extracurricular research," he said, gesturing toward the last few frames.

That part was new to me. A kid on a skateboard stakes out a familiar building. Out comes a black van. Kid follows. Black-van guy sticks something on a car. Kid rescues another kid from the car. It blows up.

I didn't know what to say. It was crazy.

"The kid and his mom lived," Micah said.

I still didn't say anything.

"I missed you," he said softly. He moved closer.

I felt terrible and wonderful. And trapped.

"Did I do something?" he asked, looking at me with those big brown eyes.

I shook my head. "My mom" was all I managed to say.

"We—I need you. I never would've done this without you." He sat down on the bed next to me, and I could feel his eyes searching my face for something.

"Don't put it all on me." I said it a little more harshly than I'd meant to.

He stood up. "No, I mean I wouldn't have stuck with this if it hadn't been for you."

Now I felt really bad.

"You don't understand, Micah." I swallowed hard. "My dad knows about *Memento*. He blocked my mobile. He grounded me. And he took it out on her."

"Oh, crap."

"And there's something else. We're moving to Los Palamos next week," I whispered. "I know I should have told you sooner."

I began to tear up, and Micah leaned in to kiss me. As our lips touched, someone knocked on the door. I slid *Memento* under the pillow while Micah spread out some other drawings on the floor. Sketches of medieval churches. They were quite spectacular.

Mom popped her head into the room.

"Dinner's in twenty minutes," she said. "Micah, you'd be wise to leave before Mr. James comes home."

Micah gathered up his church drawings. Mom stood in the doorway while I helped him stuff them into his bag.

"When does your cast come off?" Mom asked him.

The cast was all taped up.

"Not soon enough," he replied, grinning at me. "Couple weeks, ma'am," he said to my mom.

"Yours?" he asked, his grin gone.

"The same. It was just a tiny fracture." She held up her arm gingerly.

To me he said, "Wish you'd change your mind about our project, but I understand if you don't."

He left. And I felt as if all the air rushed out of the room after him.

"What was that about?" Mom asked.

"Nothing."

*   *   *

At dinner that night no one said much. Dad barely looked at me. Mom had trouble eating because the cast was on her right wrist. Dad rolled his eyes as I cut up her chicken for her. Then he pushed away from the table and told no one in particular that he was going out for drinks.

*   *   *

I dreamed the dream that night.

The ash rained down smelling of cigar smoke. It was ten to two on the silver watch. The red socks twitched. The body moaned on the pavement. He turned his face, and it was Micah. Then I heard a scream. And the sound of doors opening and closing and opening again. I looked at the body once more, and it was my mother lying on the sidewalk, clutching the book with the red words on the black cover. *Memento Nora*.

27

Little Girl Lost

Therapeutic Statement 42-03282028-11
Subject: JAMES, NORA EMILY, 15
Facility: HAMILTON DETENTION CENTER TFC-42

Winter Nomura slammed my locker shut, just barely missing my fingers.

"Micah's gone," she said. "And it's your fault." Her words were as spiky as her hair, which was all black now.

"What do you mean, gone?" I opened my locker again to get out my Spanish book.

"He never made it home yesterday." She lowered her voice. "The Village was up all night looking for him. You turned him in, didn't you?"

"I'd never," I said, closing the door a little harder than I'd intended. "But I told him I couldn't see him anymore."

"When?" she asked.

"He came over last night before dinner."

"Idiot," Winter spat out. "I told him not to go to your place. He must really like you."

She looked at me hard with those damn X-ray eyes of hers.

"Look, I believe *you* didn't turn him in," she said carefully. I could hear the inevitable *but* in her voice. And with a shiver, I knew what it was.

"But my dad probably did," I said. He must've set the house security system to alert him if Micah ever visited. I guess I should've thought of that, but I'd never dreamed Dad would do something to Micah. Me, maybe. Not Micah.

"I think I'd better go," Winter said, backing away. She had her eyes on someone or something behind me. I turned my head to get a look. It was Officer Bell. He was watching us as he searched bags across the hall. He didn't make a move toward us, though, and Winter turned as nonchalantly as she could and walked quickly down the hall in the other direction.

*   *   *

Winter was right. Micah wasn't anywhere in school. He wasn't at lunch or in the art studio. I decided to blow off Tom once and for all, skip out, and see if Micah had come home yet.

The black dog wouldn't let me past the inner gate to the Village, but through the iron bars I could see Mrs. Brooks consoling a woman in purple scrubs. I called to her, but Mrs. Brooks turned away and the dog growled at me. I ran back to school, stopping only to catch my breath at the bridge. I couldn't believe he was really gone.

The rent-a-cop barely even looked at me as he searched my bag on the way back in. The late bell rang, but I ran to the bathroom. And threw up.

As I rested my head against the cool, and hopefully clean, porcelain, I thought about staying in the bathroom until school was out. I couldn't go home yet. If I called the car service, I'd have to explain to Dad why I'd left school early. I could say I was sick, but I really couldn't face him yet. I didn't have any cash, and my only way home that second was on the school bus. Or on foot. I wasn't feeling brave enough for that. But sitting on my own in there, in the same stall where I'd stashed *Memento*s, just gave me too much time to think. About Micah. About Mom and Dad. About Winter's parents. I even thought about going to TFC and making it all just go away. For me, that is.

But I couldn't do that to Micah. Not now.

So I went to class. I avoided everyone, but one thought kept haunting me: would Micah forget me?

28

Bad Dreams and All

Therapeutic Statement *42-03282028-11*
Subject: *JAMES, NORA EMILY, 15*
Facility: *HAMILTON DETENTION CENTER TFC-42*

Dinner that night was agony. Dad was in the glossiest mood I'd seen him in for ages. He talked incessantly about the big move, which was a week from Saturday. He went on about the stuff he'd found out about the new school, the golf course, the shops in the mall. And then he mentioned that the Slaytons were next on the list to get a house. He winked at me and said that maybe I could be ungrounded for a certain dance with a certain Tom Slayton.

Mom hid behind her sunglasses. She barely ate; neither did I. All I could think about was Micah. There wasn't anything I could do for him, but it was my fault. If he hadn't come to see me, if I hadn't agreed to do the comic, if I hadn't said hi to him that day, if I hadn't spit out the pill he would've been fine. I would have been fine.

Now I thought I understood my mother. We both hoped that if we forgot things, everything would be fine. I thought again about going back to TFC. How else could I live in Dad's world, in the gated castle he wanted to keep me in, knowing what I knew without going crazy?

When I was getting ready for bed that night—dreading lying there, waiting for the dream to come—I found something under my pillow. It was the last issue of *Memento*, the one with the black vans, without words, the one Micah had brought over the night before.

I looked at the frame where the van was coming out of the parking garage, the one next to Tiffany's. I recognized that place—not the garage but the building beside it. It was 42 Randolph Street—where my dad works. Soft Target. The building and vehicles are unmarked to protect client interests, or at least that's what he'd always said.

Why would Dad's company blow up parked cars? The whole thing was ridiculous. Terrorists blew up things. That's why most people go to TFC. *To forget our cares*. To forget that the Coalition is out there stalking us. One little pill makes everything tolerable.

Then I saw it. I didn't want to see it, but there it was.

TFC is Dad's biggest client. And the worse things seem, the more attacks there are, the more money TFC and everyone else involved make.

No, that's insane. I shuddered. *That can't be the kind of security Dad provides.*

I tried to justify it in some way. Maybe Soft Target just blew up parked, empty, peopleless cars. It was the real terrorists who were still out there blowing up bookstores. Right?

Maybe. Or maybe not.

My head started to pound.

I ripped up *Memento* and threw it in the trash. Forgetting my cares actually sounded pretty good just then.

*   *   *

I had the dream again.

This time the body arced out of the window of the top floor of the bookstore. I could see the dark suit, the red socks, the silver watch, and the book as they dived toward the concrete.

I touched the book after it hit the ground. It didn't explode. I turned over the body, fully expecting it to be Micah. Or my mother. It wasn't.

It was me.

The silver watch was really a charm bracelet with a little silver purse on it. And the book didn't say *Memento Nora*. It said *Medieval Churches*.

I woke up in a cold sweat. I knew exactly what I needed to do.

I picked the pieces of *Memento* out of the trash can and taped them back together. Then I sat down at my desk and inked in the captions and dialogue. The words flowed out of me like they had the first time I told my story to Micah. And when the words were all on the paper, I nodded off. And I didn't dream.

·   ·   ·

Someone tousled my hair.

"Did you sleep at your desk?" Mom asked, concerned.

"Uh, I forgot this was due today." I tried my best to cover the drawings, but I thought she saw.

"Is that what Micah wanted you to help finish?" she asked. "Your art history project?"

I nodded. She didn't try to look at the paper, only at me.

Suddenly I wasn't sure anymore. If I got caught, it meant the Big D and the Big Pill—as Micah called it. I'd forget about the past few weeks and go back to my glossy ways, oblivious. To everything.

"Mom, why don't we go away? The two of us," I said, studying her face. "We could go to the beach, just like we did when I was younger." I saw a flicker in her eyes, like she was considering it. Or had considered it. Maybe Dad wouldn't find us this time—or even bother to look, especially if I threatened to expose him with this comic.

I felt the paper under my hands. It was so thin. It wouldn't intimidate my father.

"Beach?" Mom asked, her face crinkled with amusement. "Honey, we've never been to the beach." She laughed gently, dismissing the whole idea. "Breakfast is ready," she added as she walked into the hallway.

"Good morning, Siddy," I heard my father say as he moved past her. Then I heard him dash down the stairs. "Early morning meeting," he called right before the front door slammed shut.

The black-and-white lines of *Memento* stared at me from my desk. The black van drives out of Soft Target. Van guy sticks something on car. It blows up.

I had no appetite for breakfast.

I pulled out my history book and wrote five words in block letters across the top of chapter eleven. Just in case. I dog-eared the page so I wouldn't miss it later.

Then I stuffed the last issue of *Memento* and my copy of *Medieval Churches* into my backpack and slung it over my shoulder.

On my way downstairs I checked myself in the hall mirror. I hadn't done my hair or my makeup, and I was wearing the same clothes I had on yesterday. The old me would've never gone out like this. The new me, though, liked what she saw in the mirror, bad dreams and all.

29

The Final Piece

Therapeutic Statement 42-03282028-11
Subject: JAMES, NORA EMILY, 15
Facility: HAMILTON DETENTION CENTER TFC-42

I borrowed some money from Mom's purse and took the bus to Winter's house. She wasn't there. Mr. Yamada was sitting in the gazebo in her garden, staring at the new sculpture on the table. It was a partially constructed metal mask held in place with wires and scaffolding. Through the eyes and behind the unfinished, or maybe torn away, part of the face you could see dozens of gears. Wheels upon wheels working together. They were connected to this big red cog, almost the size of the face sitting next to it, with a wrench dangling from the nut. It was massive. And cool. And kind of creepy. Very Winter.

"The cops picked her up," he said without looking at me.

My stomach felt as if it had dropped through the floor. "They got Micah, too," I whispered. "It's all my fault."

"No, I shouldn't have trusted Bell."

"I'll probably be next," I said. "But that's okay."

Mr. Yamada looked at me, and I held up the final *Memento*. He smiled. It was the first time I'd seen him do that.

"Cops don't appreciate art," he said as he clicked a button on the remote control in his hand. The gears on the sculpture started to turn, and he lifted a flap at the base, revealing a slot.

I fed the original into the slot, and the gears started turning. The monkey wrench spun around slowly as the last ever issue of *Memento* printed out from the base of the big red cog.

It was the perfect final piece for Winter's garden.

30

But He's My Creep

Therapeutic Statement 42-03282028-11
Subject: JAMES, NORA EMILY, 15
Facility: HAMILTON DETENTION CENTER TFC-42

"Homeland High," Mr. Yamada told the cabbie as we settled into the backseat.

I'd told him he didn't need to come with me.

"I need to see my lawyer about Winter," he explained. "I'll drop you off on the way."

Neither of us wanted to talk.

An ad for the Nomura Pink Ice flickered across both of our windows. A girl a lot like me held the mobile to her ear and said, "You can never be too pink or too thin."

I felt sick, but I hugged my backpack tight. Inside, two hundred fresh copies of *Memento* waited to be released.

The cab let me out right in front of school. Mr. Yamada looked so alone sitting there in the backseat. I hitched up my backpack (and my courage) to walk up the front steps.

We'd done it before. I could do this alone, I told myself. I just needed to get past the rent-a-cops and make it to the bathrooms.

When I stepped inside, I was so busy psyching myself up that I didn't see Officer Bell standing to the side of the bag search area.

"Miss James," he said. "I need to talk to you."

The rent-a-cops looked up from their magazines. Bell opened the staff door to the garage and motioned me toward his waiting police car.

I hadn't acted fast enough. Micah and Winter must have already made their statements. I wanted to run, but my legs wouldn't move. I felt as if I were standing in a bucket of Jell-O with a two-ton weight on my back. A rent-a-cop touched something at his desk, and the front doors clicked shut, locking behind me. Trapped, I willed myself to move toward Officer Bell.

He held open the back door of his squad car for me. Somehow I got in. He flicked a couple of switches on his dashboard as he slid into the driver's seat. The windows blackened. The other switch must have been the sound damper. I couldn't hear a word he was saying into his mobile, but he was obviously arguing with someone. Then he threw the mobile on the seat and turned on the lights. We sped away from Homeland Inc. Senior High No. 17.

My only regret was that *Memento* was still in my backpack. My friends would never know about the vans or the car bombings. Neither would I.

As Bell's big gray car hurtled me toward the Big D, I

imagined the old me waking to find she'd hit the jackpot. A glossy life behind the gates. A new house. A seemingly happy family. The right friends. Her own car. And a date to the prom with Tom Slayton.

I felt sorry for her, especially when she'd read what I'd written across the top of the chapter on the Renaissance in her history book.

YOUR FATHER BEATS YOUR MOTHER.

I hoped that was enough to keep Mom (and the old Nora) safe. Would I believe me? I don't know. Maybe I can leave some things out of my statement before I get the Big Pill, some things for the old me to hang on to.

Winter and Micah must have omitted a lot in their statements or else Bell would have been arrested, too. Well, not if he'd been working undercover and narced on the whole Memory Loss Support Group. Mr. Yamada was right. We shouldn't have trusted him.

Bell slowed the car and parked.

"Did you turn in the whole MLSG?" I blurted out as he opened the car door. "They trusted you."

Officer Bell pointed toward a building. That's when I noticed where we were. It wasn't a police station. It was the same alley, the same back door to the same church where we'd met the MLSG. Southside Methodist Church.

Inside were the same macaroni paintings, the same burned coffee smells, and the same folding chairs as before. The chairman, Ms. Curtis, and two other members waited for us in the little kitchen. The librarian, to my surprise, rushed to meet us. The others stayed put, sipping their coffee and watching us over the white brims of their Styrofoam cups. Ms. Curtis hugged me lightly, pulling away after a few seconds as if she was embarrassed by her feelings.

"Does that answer your question?" Officer Bell asked. "I'm sorry we couldn't get Winter and Micah in time," he added quietly. The worn Formica breakfast bar stood between us and the coffee klatch in the kitchen. Under the counter, Ms. Curtis gently took his hand.

"Then why haven't you or Ms. Curtis been picked up?" I asked. "Or them? Or Mr. Yamada? He thinks you turned in Winter." I wondered if he'd seen Bell grab me through the plate glass doors of the school. Or if he was already on the way to his lawyer's.

"Katie and I were ready to make a run for it as soon as we heard Micah was gone," Bell said, staring at some random fleck in the countertop. "But then a friend at the detention center told me that someone ordered the kids held without statement." He looked up at me, anger in his eyes. "They're kids. It should be a simple erase and release job. I tried to call Koji, but he wouldn't answer."

I had a cold feeling in the pit of my stomach. And I was suddenly conscious of the cool silver bracelet dangling on my wrist. "My father?" I asked.

Bell nodded. "He doesn't want them to implicate you."

Or screw his career. Mom had changed hers because it was hurting his.

"But how can he stop them from talking?" I asked. "Don't the police run Detention?" Did Dad have that much power?

"Soft Target runs the Hamilton Detention Center for Homeland Inc.," Bell replied.

"Which is owned by TFC," Ms. Curtis added.

"Oh," I whispered. My dad ran the Big D. And his people blew up shit. For the company that would help you forget about it with one little white pill. TFC was the one with so much power. I took a deep breath and tried to absorb it all. It didn't work. I couldn't quite wrap my head around Dad making his living—*our* living—this way. And *he* was the one holding Micah and Winter. Another thought popped into my head. "If Micah hasn't talked yet, why did Winter get picked up?"

"He made a call to her before he was detained," Bell said. "About a printer."

"Damn." It's a monitored network. Micah had said it himself. And he'd forgotten it when it counted the most. That was probably my fault, too.

"Their detention also protects us," the chairman said. He put down his coffee cup and walked around the counter to where Bell, Ms. Curtis, and I were standing. The others continued to sip their coffees and watch us warily. "If they don't talk, no one will know about us—which is why you cannot hand out any more of those comics. You cannot risk going to Detention, young lady," Mr. Carver said, putting his hand on my shoulder. "For our sakes and your own."

Officer Bell snorted, but I felt an odd sense of relief flooding through me. The backpack felt lighter. Maybe I had no business endangering these people. Maybe I should ditch *Memento*, leave it to the adults, and get on with my life.

"It's a pity about your friends, though." The chairman closed his hand on my bag.

A pity? I drew back. I could see Bell staring at the floor, not wanting to look at me. Then I got it. If Micah and Winter were being held without the possibility of them telling their stories—which was the only way to erase their memories—then they could be in Detention indefinitely. And all because of me.

My dad didn't want TFC to know that his little princess was involved—and that he'd been unable to stop it. That would ruin everything for him. No big contracts. No house in the compound. No money.

So my friends could sit in the Big D not telling anybody anything for years. Just like Winter's parents. Maybe that's why they're still there. Somebody didn't want them to talk, either. I backed away from the chairman, clutching my backpack.

"You—we—can't leave Winter and Micah in Detention forever," I said. The chairman's face told me he could. Maybe. His eyes darted to the other members in the kitchen. They looked to Ms. Curtis, who gripped Bell's hand tightly. I turned to him. "If I tell my story, would the authorities have to hear Micah's and Winter's? You said it should be a simple erase and release case, right?"

Bell didn't answer for a moment. I could see him turning the possibilities over in his head. "You know you'd have to get caught red-handed, right?" he said slowly. "Otherwise your father could continue to protect you." He paused again. "Your father wouldn't hold *you* in Detention forever, would he?"

My dad might be a lot of things—ambitious, controlling, cruel even—but deep down I know he loves me. I think he even loves Mom, in his own awful way.

However, it would certainly be embarrassing for him if his biggest client found out that his daughter wrote (and distributed) *Memento*—and he covered it up by keeping two other kids on ice. Okay, Dad is definitely a creep, but he's *my* creep. I had to gamble that he loves his princess enough not to tuck her away forever behind bars just to cover his own ass.

And the story was important enough to take the risk. Kids needed to know TFC was blowing up shit to keep us scared. Scared enough to forget but not too frightened to stop spending money. I thought of Winter's crab sculpture, scrambling along, weighed down by its shopping bag shell, unable to break free.

I shook my head. "Take me back to school."

The chairman and the other MLSG members started to object, but Bell quieted them with a glare.

"Hold on," Bell said to me. "We have to be sure your father can't still *fix* things. . . ." He trailed off.

I knew what he was thinking. Dad could still get me out before I made a statement if there wasn't a lot of attention around my arrest.

"We need witnesses," I finished for him.

Ms. Curtis nodded. "The phone tree," she said, staring

intently at the chairman as if daring him to object. Without breaking that stare, she explained to me that MLSG members know the numbers of only three other members. When there's a meeting, you call three, then each of those three call three, and so on. "These are my three," she said as she shifted her gaze from the chairman to the MLSG folks in the kitchen. After a moment—to their credit it didn't take them too long—her three put down their cups and joined us.

"We've got some calls to make," Bell said, "before I take Nora back." The chairman grunted, about to cut in, but Bell pressed on. "The kids only know me, the chairman, and Ms. Curtis by name. Everyone else can just lie low when this is done. Katie and I will disappear together after I drop off Nora." Turning to me, he tried to smile but couldn't.

I also failed miserably at the smiling thing. I was so not glossy—and I couldn't even fake it anymore.

The chairman, Bell, and the others made their calls. Ms. Curtis, I noticed, had slipped out the back into the stairwell to make a call. As I walked toward her, I heard her say, "Just give me five minutes."

When she came back in, I said, "I thought those were your contacts, Ms. Curtis." I motioned to the others still on their phones. I said it loud enough for Bell to hear.

The librarian snapped her phone shut. "Just calling work." She brushed past me.

"Something wrong, Katie?" Bell asked as he crossed the room.

"We need to get out of here," she said quickly. "We need to get *her* back to school." She flashed a strained smile at him as she herded us toward the door. "We need to go *now*."

Then we heard footsteps overhead. Lots of them. They scattered as if they were searching every room up there.

"No!" Ms. Curtis said angrily. "They were supposed to wait until we'd gone."

"What?" Bell had stopped with one hand on my shoulder. The color was gone from his face. He looked like someone had shot him.

I'd trusted her, too. I'd spilled my guts about something I hadn't shared with any other person besides Micah. And I hadn't told him everything. She'd listened and reassured me that I'd done the right thing. Of course, she knew what was going to happen all along. But if I'd listened to her, I wouldn't be here now.

"I'm sorry, Doug," she said, her eyes begging him to understand, her hands still pushing us toward the back door. "I had to." She looked at me as tears welled up in her eyes. "I was trying to do the right thing." I could see her story there. My father or someone else had gotten to her. Maybe Dad had made the connection between us that day he came to school. And maybe he'd asked her to keep an eye on me and my friends or narc on hers. Or else. "I did it for us," she said, her voice trembling as she met Bell's eyes. "For your job and mine. For our future together. And for my mother. They said they'd let her go."

Bell backed away from her. Ms. Curtis looked desperate,

like everything she loved was blowing up in her face. And I guess it was.

The footsteps got closer to the top of the stairs.

"They don't know you're here, Nora," she said. "I just agreed to rat out the group leaders." She gave us one last push toward the door. "I'll stall them as long as I can," she added quietly, then she darted up the stairs.

"So will we," the chairman said as he and two other MLSG men moved to block the stairwell. "Go."

Bell didn't budge. He stood there staring after Ms. Curtis for a long moment—one we didn't have. We could hear her talking to the police or whoever they were. I poked my head out into the alley. Nobody. I tugged hard on Bell's arm, and he finally sprang into action. We dashed to his car. He punched in the ignition code, but nothing happened.

"Damnit," he swore, and then pointed to the sticker on the windshield. "We've been deactivated."

I didn't know what that meant, but I could see a bigger danger down the alley. Several blocks away, a black van was parked across the alley exit. I glanced over my shoulder and saw a similar van blocking the entrance.

"I'm sorry, kid," Bell said. He smacked the steering wheel with his fist.

Then something in the car crackled, and a muffled voice said, "The side alley on your left is clear."

Bell fished an old walkie-talkie out from under his seat. "Copy that," he said, holding down one of the buttons.

"Officer Bell?" I said slowly, again pointing toward the black van in front of us. He looked up and saw it, too.

A guy in a black uniform was walking slowly toward us, his machine gun raised, pointing straight at us. "Get out of the car," the man barked. He was still a couple hundred feet away.

"Follow my lead," Bell said as he tucked his walkie-talkie into my backpack. "And when I say *run*, run like hell down that side alley." He nodded his head toward an alley on the left. It was a few yards in front of the car.

We got out of the car with our hands in the air. Bell had his badge in one hand. He yelled that he was a cop and that he was taking me in for truancy. We walked slowly forward as Bell ranted at the guy in black about disabling a police vehicle and interfering with an officer of the law. As he got closer, I could see the man's uniform was as unmarked as the van. "Let's see some ID!" Bell called as we drew even with that side alley. Bell stopped walking, but he didn't stop talking. "Who do you work for?" he shouted. Then he said to me real low, almost like a growl, "Run."

I did. My backpack in tow, I took off down that alley like my nightmares were chasing me. Behind me I heard Bell yell at the Soft Target guy—who else could he be?—about costing him his collar. Then I heard a scuffle. I kept running, but I didn't know where I was going. The alley stunk. It was nothing but dumpsters, trash, and fire escapes.

"Hide," the voice in my backpack crackled. I ducked behind a particularly smelly trash bin. I could hear the screech of tires and running. A figure in black shot past where I was hiding. A dark figure swung down a fire escape and knocked the Soft Target guy to the ground. The guy didn't get up. Mr. Yamada, in his black tracksuit, stood in front of me. Sasuke indeed.

"We need to get you to school," he said, not at all out of breath. "It's only a few blocks down on your right, over the King footbridge. Hide on the other side of that dumpster." Mr. Yamada pointed toward the mouth of the alley. "And wait for my signal." With that, he scrambled back up the fire escape and onto the roof in one fluid motion.

Micah would have loved it. Too bad I won't remember to tell him.

The guy on the ground moaned. I scrambled toward the spot Mr. Yamada had shown me.

"It's clear. Turn right," Mr. Yamada said through the walkie-talkie in my bag, his voice barely loud enough to hear above the street noise. I imagined him leaping across rooftops and swinging from ledges up above as I scurried along the street. When he told me to duck into a doorway or hide behind a car, I did without even thinking about it. And soon the King footbridge was in sight.

I stopped on it for a moment to catch my breath and watch the traffic stream underneath me. No black vans among them.

"You don't have to do this," a voice said beside me. Mr. Yamada stood there in the flesh once more. This time he was a little winded.

"I do," I told him, and started walking.

He took the walkie-talkie from my bag and followed

me without saying another word. And then Koji Yamada melted into the crowd that was beginning to form in front of the school.

Score one for the phone tree, I thought. I could feel their eyes on me as I pushed through the front doors.

The security guards searched my bag and then watched me walk down the hall into a crowd of my friends. I opened my big, hollow book on medieval churches and started handing out copies of *Memento* as fast as I could. My girls looked shocked; but as the security guards started running toward us, Maia and Abby grabbed handfuls of paper and started throwing them in the air. So did Tom Slayton. Other kids jumped for pieces of paper before they ran off to catch their buses or go to practice. I stood there, paper raining down on me, until I felt a hand on my shoulder.

I turned to face the rent-a-cops. Behind them I could see that the crowd on the steps outside had grown bigger. At the front, Mr. Yamada was flanked by several MLSG members I sort of recognized and a striking-looking tattooed woman in a corset and jeans whom I'd never seen before. And beside her stood Micah's Mrs. Brooks, gripping the leash of the big black dog.

Evidently you can't monitor all the people all the time.

The front doors locked, and one of the security guards shoved me through the staff door into the parking garage.

"Damnit, where's Bell?" he said, motioning for the other guard to get the car.

And just as rent-a-cop number two ran toward the first

parking level, an elegant, short-haired woman with a tiger claw tattoo peeking out from underneath her cap sleeve stepped between the door and me. She stuck a Channel 5 Action News camera in my face and asked me what this was all about.

So I told her.

Everything.

Well, everything I could get out before the rent-a-cop came back with the car.

Detention,
the Big D Variety

And that brings us to the here and now. It's ten past two on I-don't-know-what day, and I've told you the story of *Memento*, of me and Winter and Micah. I'm sure they've told you theirs, too. Well, I hope they have. And you know it's the truth because you gave me a shot of something to make me blab like this.

My mom is sitting here behind her shades listening to every word. Trembling. White. Ashen, really. Definitely not glossy. But all there. She'll hold my hand while you give me the Big Pill so I'll forget everything that I've just said. No doubt you'll make sure I swallow this time. Then you'll give her a pill, and she'll forget all about this, too.

And we'll live glossily ever after in Los Palamos.

Epilogue:
Renaissance

MICAH

I felt like I'd been in a coma for days, weeks maybe. Then it was like I'd come to and found myself on the bus with Mom. Home Security Depot was hawking some new crap in front of me while I was plugged into my earbuds, the Lo-Fi Strangers' newest tune roaring through my foggy brain. Next, some Channel 5 Action News chick reported on an investigation into a security company. Blah-blah-blah. I closed my eyes again.

"This is us," Mom said.

I stumbled out of the bus after her, still not feeling quite all there. It wasn't our stop.

Mom grinned and dangled something in front of me. A key card. She pointed to the building across the street. "Third floor," she said. "Our stuff's already inside." She tossed me the key. "Even your sketch pads."

WINTER

A cab let us off at the corner of Eighth and Day. My brain felt like pudding. The last thing I remembered, I told Grandfather, was working on the sculpture garden in the backyard.

Sculpture garden? he asked as if he didn't have a clue what I was talking about. We pressed our way through the secret door in the back fence, through the Sasuke course, and through the bamboo gates into my garden.

Grandfather didn't say a word as he took in the Paw-ing Man, the Flailing-Arm Windmill, and the Shopping-Bag Crab. Those, I remembered creating. That masked thing with the monkey wrench and the gears, though, was a complete mystery to me. It was like a stranger had invaded my garden and finished it for me.

I wanted to be that person.

NORA

Mom and I walked for blocks without saying a word. Then she stopped, spit something out on the sidewalk, and ground it under her Italian leather heel. Right in front of the Starbucks next to TFC No. 23. Right in front of a word— *MEMENTO*—spray painted in red.

"Thank you, Nora," she said, looking all sad and smiley at me.

"For what?" I had no idea what she was talking about. The last thing I remembered clearly was getting in the car this morning to go shopping with her. I checked my mobile. Nearly four weeks had gone by.

"I'll tell you on the way to the beach." She flashed her mobile at me. Her TFC point balance was zero. "I knew I was saving up for something."

When I asked if Dad would be joining us, she just smiled again and said, "Oh, he's going to be a bit tied up at work now. The whole company, your father especially, is in hot water over this black-van thing."

I didn't ask what she meant. I was busy admiring the glossy silver bracelet, with its little purse charm, dangling from my wrist.

We stopped by the house to pick up a few things. Mom insisted that I pack my history book. She said I had an exam on the Renaissance when we got back. How dreary.

Later, while we munched popcorn shrimp at this cute café by the sea, Mom told me this crazy story about me and some kids named Micah and Winter and a comic book (of all things) we created.

It didn't sound like me at all.